THE MIDNIGHT RIDE

A Becky Bing Mystery

By

Gordon Mathieson

Published by GMCI Books

This is a work of fiction and is produced from the author's imagination. People, places, and things mentioned in this novel are used in a fictional manner.

ISBN: 9781478190127

Cover design and photograph by Kathy Crowley

Editor: Erin Potter

Printed in the United States of America

ACKNOWLEDGEMENTS

There are many people who helped me along the journey of this, my third, Becky Bing novel. Some of this assistance came in the form of editing, research consultation, others' expert advice on how to fine-tune my Mandarin translation, and finally, with the cover design and presentation.

First of all, I want to give a big shout out to my editor, Erin Potter of Shamrock Editing, who has helped me with many of my books, not only with her technical skills, but also for her unfettered opinions on how the story might read more smoothly and become more appealing for readers of all ages.

I want to thank Leo Anthony, President and CEO of Asian Boston Media Group. He is someone who has dedicated his career and life to advance the opportunities for the Asian American community in Boston, New England, and New York. Leo has always made himself available for questions I might have for him. He and his associates have significantly helped the Asian community in many disciplines with Asian Boston Radio, TV, Music, Modeling, and other services.

When Leo learned how my purpose was similar to his; to bridge the Asian and American cultures by providing professional opportunities of all stripes, he graciously invited me into his sphere of effort and to participate where appropriate.

Dr. Junying Kirk, of Birmingham, UK, a talented author originally from China, has successfully drawn readers into a world we now understand better since she courageously penned her sensitive and compelling books. She reviewed my Mandarin dialogue, suggesting modifications where applicable.

Likewise, Jessie Ahern, originally from Taiwan, and my local Chinese Language instructor here on Cape Cod, has been most helpful editing my translations. I thank her for her patience and enthusiasm.

Kathy Crowley has helped me design and capture the image I want for several of my book covers. I owe her a great deal of gratitude for her artistic skill.

As always, I want to acknowledge my best friend and wife, Ann, who has been with me since we met at eighteen years of age. Her patience, consultation, and support of my writing still brings us closer—even when my mind is in a distant place working on a project such as this one.

Listen my children and you shall hear,

Of the midnight ride of Paul Revere…..

From the poem, *Paul Revere's Ride*,
by Henry Wordsworth Longfellow (1860)

CHAPTER ONE

The sweet aroma of freshly baked, chocolate-chip cookies wafted into her nostrils as she stepped through the front door entrance. The inviting scent fired up hunger pangs after a long day of high school classes followed by her part-time job.

As she stepped across the living room, the grandfather clock chimed nine-thirty.

"Hey, I'm home, Mom!" Becky yelled out. "Going up to change but I'll be right back down for your cookies!"

Becky headed up toward the staircase centered inside the Bing home.

"You just had a phone call from an, ah…rather interesting girl.''

"Oh, really, who was it?"

"She's someone you never met before but wants you to call her back tonight no matter how late," her mom yelled out. "I've got the number for you to call when you come back downstairs."

Becky followed her typical routine; skipping steps up the carpeted, winding staircase. With her heavy book bag strapped over her shoulders the routine climb was an intense physical workout for her five-foot-three inch frame.

Inside her bedroom, she kicked off her sandals and unyoked the heavy bag. She quickly stripped down to her bra and panties then pulled on a pink T-shirt over her head. The front of the novelty shirt was adorned with a panda bear eating bamboo shoots and expressing a silly but satisfied smile.

She slipped into a pair of plaid boxer shorts, making up one of her typical bedtime ensembles. Within minutes, her bare feet padded back down the staircase heading toward the source of aromatic sweetness.

"Hi, Mom!" The petite, seventeen-year-old rose up on tiptoes to give her mother a quick hug and peck on the cheek. "You have no idea how freakin' glad I am that today's Friday! It's been a long week at school and nothing but bitchy customers today at the store. My God! It must be a full moon tonight!"

"I hear ya, Sweetie," Mrs. Bing replied, watching her daughter with a curled grin on her lips.

"I so need my trip up to Boston next week. It'll be like a well-deserved vacation!"

Her eyes then focused on the cooling rack set upon the kitchen counter. She morphed into a theatrical persona imitating a British Victorian maiden.

"But now, I shall reap the rewards of my labor! I feel like I'll faint if I don't get something into my stomach." Her long, slender fingers nimbly plucked a warm cookie from the metal rack. Without hesitation, she sank her teeth into the inviting sweetness, biting off a morsel.

"Here, Beck, take this before I forget." The attractive blonde, blue-eyed Alicia Bing handed her only child a piece of paper from a notepad. "This girl called about a half-hour ago. She told me her name's Samantha Rawlings. She's one of the twelve national scholarship winners, like you. Evidently, she's traveling by train on her way to Boston for next week's events."

"Hmm. Did she say where she was from?"

"Yeah, well, she told me she left her grandparents' home in Evansville, Indiana earlier in the day. I didn't tell her that you were driving up to Boston on Sunday morning. Oh, and by the way, Dad called this afternoon, too. He got an early flight from his AMA Conference tomorrow afternoon. He'll be home by dinner. You know how he wants to wish you well before your first trip away from home on your own!"

Becky sipped from a glass of milk and mused for a moment about her doting father. It triggered an affectionate grin and deepened the dimples on her petite, bronze-toned face.

"Thanks, Mom. I'll give this…ah, Samantha whoever, a call right now."

She then headed for the living room, finger-tapping digits into her cell. As the connection rang, she plopped down on the sofa. A girl's voice answered.

"Samantha?" said Becky.

"Hey, Becky, how are you? Thanks for the call back." Her accent authenticated she wasn't from New England. "So, you're one of the American History scholarship winners too!"

"Yeah, my mom told me you're one of the 'chosen twelve'. So, where are you right now?"

"Ah, I haven't a clue. I guess somewhere near Pennsylvania. But I'm getting off at the New Haven train station for a few hours tomorrow. And…I thought if you had some free time we could meet up before the formal stuff begins up in Boston."

Becky paused before responding. She was surprised at the bold request from someone she didn't know. But she also understood Midwesterners were more open to strangers than the stoic, reserved New Englanders.

"Huh? Ah…how long is your layover in New Haven, Samantha?"

“Oh, please call me Sam. I prefer it to Samantha. All my friends call me Sam.”

“Okay, Sam it is!”

“It doesn’t really matter. There are several trains leaving from New Haven to Boston that I can jump on in the afternoon. But I did want to see the Yale campus since I’ve applied there.”

“Oh, really? Yale, huh?”

“To be honest though, I really want to attend Northwestern in Illinois. But I thought I’d leave a little early for this scholarship gig and check out the ‘Ivy’ in New Haven. And, I thought since you live nearby in North Haven, we might meet up and have lunch or something before my train leaves for Boston.”

Becky still deferred making any commitment.

“Ah, what time are you arriving in New Haven?”

“The train’s scheduled to arrive at nine-fifteen in the morning.”

Becky’s brain went through ambivalent and rapid machinations. But her innate human generosity overruled any fleeting, selfish thoughts. Plans of sleeping in late on a leisurely Saturday morning instantly vanished.

“Ah, yeah. Okay, Sam. Tell you what. I’ll drive to the train station and be in the waiting area. And if you’d like, I can give you a quick tour of the campus since my dad is….”

“….a Yale professor. He’s a world-known surgeon and Chairman of the Orthopedics Department,” Sam said, finishing Becky’s sentence almost as if she had rehearsed it.

Becky took in a long, deep breath and exhaled slowly after the obnoxious interruption. It was her personal, conditioned routine at moments like this. The instinctive exercise helped her maintain balance, suppress anger, and enabled her not to lose her cool.

“Well, it…it seems you’ve done your research on my family,” she remarked.

"Yeah. I, ah, read a little about your father and your mom in the bio profile you submitted to the scholarship committee and that got me curious to do a little more research on my own. In fact, I have a copy of all of the scholarship winners' profiles in the program with me on this trip. Did you get a copy of the program, Becky?"

"Well, yeah, I got the whole packet in the mail a couple of weeks ago notifying us that we had won the competition and the scholarship award. But, I must admit, I only skimmed over all that stuff then. I'll take a better look at it before I head up to Boston on Sunday morning."

"Okay then! I look forward to meeting with you tomorrow morning at nine. Goodnight for now!"

"Hey! Wait, wait, Sam, don't hang up! How the heck will I recognize you at the train station?"

A deep, throaty chuckle resonated from Sam Rawlings at the other end of the connection.

"Oh, hell, Becky, you can't miss me, simply by the color of my hair!"

"Huh? The color of your hair? What…what color hair do you have?"

"It's green, a frosted neon-green."

CHAPTER TWO

After the call, Becky ambled into the family room by way of the kitchen to snatch up just one more cookie. Her mind was still unsettled after the surprise call and now the impromptu encounter scheduled for early on Saturday morning.

"So, did you talk with Samantha from Evansville?" Mrs. Bing asked.

"Ah, yeah. We just spoke."

"How'd it go? Was she nice?"

Becky paused before answering. She plopped down on the sofa folding her legs beneath her.

"Well, she wants to meet me tomorrow morning during her layover at the New Haven train station."

Alicia Bing stared at her daughter before speaking.

"Oh, that's interesting. And…how do you feel about that?"

"Hmm. I'm really not too sure yet. But I think I'm gonna check her out a bit. I'm going upstairs now to read her bio profile in the scholarship packet."

"Hey, I'd like to read those profiles sometime too! This Samantha seemed to know a lot about me and your father from what you wrote in your bio piece."

Becky's bare feet abruptly stopped then pivoted around toward her mother.

"Oh, really? What did she say about you and Dad?"

"Well, she really blabbered on when I answered the call. It was sort of a nervous chatter. She already knew that your father is a well-known orthopedic surgeon from the Yale Medical School. But she also told me she read somewhere how I was a former trial attorney before becoming a law professor. She alluded to some celebrities I had represented years ago when we lived in New York City."

"You're kidding me!"

"Yeah, I was really surprised at that. That history goes back some time, before your dad and I adopted you from China as an infant. But what really struck me was she also knew I was once a 'wannabe actress'. That goes way back to my days as a law school student. And, she just rattled things off so quickly, talking non-stop. It just blew me away. So, tell me dear, what exactly did you write in that biography profile for the scholarship application?"

Becky was dumbstruck.

"Mom, I didn't include any of that personal stuff in my bio! I'll show it to you. I just described my life as a student and very little about our family. I wrote nothing about you being a former trial lawyer or about any people you had represented. And, there was absolutely nothing about your wanting to become an actress!"

"Well, she did some extensive research on our family on her own."

"My God! I had forgotten all about you telling me that part of your life! This…this Evansville chick has done some serious 'GOOGLING' about the Bing family of North Haven, Connecticut."

Mother and daughter momentarily stared at each other without saying a word. Mrs. Bing broke the silence with some diplomacy.

"Well, maybe she's someone who needs to know more about those she'll be spending time with away from home. You high school seniors will be living together up in Boston for a week. Maybe she's anxious about meeting new kids, especially being away from her family and friends. Perhaps the more she knows about you, a potential buddy, might make her feel better."

Becky looked directly into her mom's eyes. Not a word was spoken because neither one of them believed for a second what Mrs. Bing had said.

"Well, two can play that game! I think I'll check her out online and do my own research before we meet tomorrow morning. But I can tell you already, I don't like her freakin' hair."

"Huh? What's wrong with her hair, Sweetie?"

"It's the color; it's some kind of electric-green."

Mrs. Bing arched her eyebrows. "Oh, well, that's, ah, interesting."

Becky returned upstairs to her bedroom, cookie in one hand and a glass of milk in the other. She sat at her desk and pulled out a professionally printed packet with an impressive label, *The Annual American History Scholarship Program.*

She quickly flipped to the student profile biography section of the thin, glossy program booklet. Each page had a header with student's name, high school and hometown, and some demographics followed by a page of text. There were no photos since none were allowed to be submitted when applying to the national scholarship competition.

Becky thumbed to the personal page for "Samantha Iris Rawlings." She quickly skimmed over the few paragraphs of her bio.

She learned that Samantha had come from a modest family in Iowa and had been orphaned at a young age. Her grandparents in Evansville, Indiana had raised her and her brother since she was very young.

Her grandmother had been a middle school teacher before retiring to help her husband run a large farm.

Sam attended public schools and did well academically. In her junior year, she was accepted into the National Honor Society and had won competitive awards in creative writing. Besides her academic courses, she was heavily involved with community projects and the Four H club.

The honor student also mentioned how she was close to her only sibling, a younger brother, Glen.

Samantha was quoted in her bio saying she'd rather "act than do anything else." But she had a better plan for a more stable career. She had aspirations of becoming a history teacher at the middle or high school level. She had already written a stage screenplay parody on the Pilgrims landing in America.

According to her last paragraph, she was still undecided as to the college of her choice.

Becky slowly re-read the page then thought about the vague summary of Samantha Rawlings' life. Stretching out on the bed, she looked up at the ceiling, and thought.

There's not too much there. It appears she had a tougher time than most, without parents. She and her younger brother lived with the grandparents from an early age. I'm sure she'll do well in college, especially with her bent toward researching information. It sounds like she really needed this scholarship to pay for her college education. And without photographs of any of the twelve students, I still don't know what she looks like. I'll have to wait for that "pleasant surprise" tomorrow at the train station.

A familiar ring-tone broke up her private thoughts.

"Hey what's going on?" her boyfriend, Jake, asked.

Becky talked non-stop for several minutes, barely taking time to breathe. She described the unexpected phone call from the mysterious Midwestern student.

She also told him about Sam's extra personal research on the Bing family.

"Hey, that's all dope, Beck! At least you'll already know at least one of the kids before you get up to Boston. It'll be cool."

Becky smiled at her boyfriend's consistent upbeat and positive attitude.

"Yeah, I suppose you're right. Who knows? She may turn out to be cool."

"Hey, I don't have any work tomorrow. I just have to help my mom do some things. Maybe I can connect with you guys in New Haven and get to meet her too."

"Yeah, that'd be great! And, let's go somewhere afterward. I just need to be home in time for dinner."

"Sweet! You know, Beck, I really want some time with you in the afternoon. The weather's gonna be good so maybe we can go for a nice long walk."

"Sounds great! We've never been away since we started going together almost six months ago. But this scholarship is really a big deal. Besides being prestigious and nationally recognized, the award is for $10,000 over my four years of college."

"Really? That is so cool!"

"Yeah, but in order for us to receive the award we must be present at the week-long event in Boston. It's mandatory. No show, no dough."

"What are you going to do for a week up there?"

"We get to visit nearby colleges, attend lectures, go on tours of historical places, museums and stuff like that. It's kinda like a week's paid vacation on top of the scholarship. Since the award is for an American History scholarship, it's held in Boston each year."

"Cool!" Jake interjected.

"Then on Thursday night, after a formal dinner, each of us must deliver a five-minute synopsis of our research papers to a larger audience."

"Who will be in the audience?"

"I guess some American History professors from universities around New England."

"Oh, I know you. You'll do fine!"

"And get this! The first scholarship check for our first year in college is presented to us at the end of the week. There are no strings attached. Each student can use the $2,500 check each academic year to spend on anything we want; for tuition, books, or even personal expenses."

"Hey, that's not bad for just one research paper. I remember you had put a lot of work into it. You submitted your entry just soon after I met you."

"Yep."

"You know, Becky, I thought that whole thing was kind of weird. You told me the competition was to take a small piece of American History and dispute it through your documented research. I remember you chose Paul Revere's Ride from Boston to Concord on that famous night that kicked off the Revolutionary War in 1775. You told me your paper addressed how reality and legend blurred the events of what really happened during that famous April night."

Becky chuckled.

"Actually, my research turned out to be a lot of fun! It was a little like solving a mystery. It all started when I re-read the famous Paul Revere's Ride poem by Longfellow. While I was reading it, I became curious and started cross-checking with respectable researchers. Then I looked at some school text books. Some discrepancies surfaced between the academic research and the poem."

"And what did you find?"

"Well, what got me going on this was that the school textbooks drew on Longfellow's poem as their reference source instead of the facts. So a lot of what is printed in our American History books is based on the words of a creative poet!"

"But that was just a poem, for God's sake!"

"I know, I know. Good ol' Longfellow had literary license to write whatever he damn well wanted. But I found that publishers had 'borrowed' his rhyming poetry and used it as historical fact. These are the same books we all studied in our American History classes. So, my research paper analyzed the historical accounts of what really happened and not those based on a poem."

Jake chuckled. "I'm not surprised you're one of the dozen national winners. One thing I know about you is once you put your mind to something, you get to the bottom of it, no matter what!"

She gave a teasing chuckle. "Geez, with all that flattery, it sounds like you want something from me, Jake."

There was a pause.

"I do want something," he said. "I definitely want to see you, tomorrow. Listen, I'll text you and find out where you and this…this green-haired, mystery girl are at the time, so we can meet up. Then after she gets back on the train, we can go somewhere in the afternoon."

"Sounds like a plan."

Before slipping into bed, she read more of the Scholarship Program package she had only skimmed earlier. The official program guide also outlined the student dress code, social rules, and underscored that alcohol or illegal drugs would not be tolerated. Any infractions were grounds for immediate termination of the scholarship and dismissal from the program in Boston.

Becky put the program away and slid under the bedcovers. She lay awake thinking about the week ahead of her. She was anxious and excited about being away from her parents for the first time in her young adult life. It would be exciting to be in Boston, so different from her quiet North Haven suburb. She also planned on visiting the Harvard University campus in nearby Cambridge. Her application to that school had already been submitted to be considered for Early Admission acceptance.

Before turning off the light, she sent a text message to Jake.

Hey! Gonna miss you lots next week, Babe! I just checked out the program again. Excited about Boston! Lots to do up there. But there's something else. Can't explain it but some weird voice in my head keeps telling me I'm in for a challenge next week. Not sure what it means. I hope it's good!

xxxxoooo

Goodnight!

CHAPTER THREE

The next morning Becky woke up early. After putting on her jogging gear, she stepped outside for her usual three-mile run. The iPhone provided her favorite tunes while she ran her circuit around the affluent Beechwood Knoll neighborhood. The cool morning temperature made for a refreshing loop as she checked her stopwatch, finishing up in front of her house.

After showering and dressing in a shirt-blouse and blue jeans, she bounced down the stairs to find her mom in the kitchen. Mrs. Bing, still dressed in her robe and pajamas, was making tea.

"Hey, it's a nice September day out there, Mom; a little chilly now but the sun will warm us up later."

"Yeah. In fact, while you're out, I'm going to dig up the gladiola bulbs from the flower beds to take in for the winter." She looked down at her cell phone. "Oh, it's Dad. He just texted he'll be home sometime in the late afternoon. Oh, and just to let you know, I'm making pork medallions with stir-fry veggies for dinner."

"Great! You know it's one of my favorites!"

Becky smiled at her mother who enjoyed balancing her household with her part-time teaching job at nearby Quinnipiac University Law School.

"I'll try to be home to help out, but I'm seeing Jake later today. He's meeting me in New Haven while I'm with the Midwestern detective, better known as Samantha from Evansville."

Her mother chuckled at the comment.

With the brightness of the Saturday morning, Becky grabbed her Ray Ban aviator sunglasses and slid them over her ears. She liked the sexy pair of shades although they covered a good part of her pixie-like face.

After slipping on her Nike nylon jacket, she kissed her mother goodbye and stepped outside.

Within minutes she was backing her older model Volvo out of the driveway. The car had belonged to her mom, who had opted for a new model and given this one to Becky on her recent seventeenth birthday.

There was only light traffic on the fifteen minute drive into New Haven on this Saturday morning. She pulled into the station's circular driveway and parked at the short term lot. When she stepped inside the station, she saw many students milling about inside the cavernous lobby. Some were arriving into the college city while others, no doubt, were escaping for the weekend to be with family and friends.

When she glanced up at the huge electronic board listing arrivals and departures, she saw that the train originating in Evansville via Pittsburgh, Pennsylvania was still "on time."

Becky sat on one of the long, teakwood, high-back benches. Just as she inserted her ear buds, she spotted a young woman pulling a wheeled, black suitcase into the huge, marble-floored waiting room. A trendy, Brood-styled cap topped her bright, green-colored hair.

The slender young woman wore straight-cut blue jeans with a light-grey sweatshirt under a black, cotton vest. *Purdue U.* was printed on her shirt. Black leather military boots made her look taller than she was. Most of her face was masked with large, Hollywood style, rose-colored sunglasses.

Becky stood up and waved to her, yelling out, "Sam, Sam, over here!"

Samantha spotted her, smiled, and stepped briskly across the marble floor; her steps echoing throughout the lobby.

"Hi! You must be Becky!"

"I am!"

Becky extended her hand to shake, but Samantha ignored it. She stepped closer to embrace the shorter girl from Connecticut with an enthusiastic bear-hug.

"I'm so happy you could meet me! Oh, I do hope you didn't think me too forward asking you to meet me here. I mean, it was a great opportunity to meet someone before getting to Boston. And…you being familiar with Yale's campus—well, that is just an added plus!"

Becky watched as the taller girl talked with such drama in her voice. With theatrical energy, fluid hand movements, and dancing eyebrows, she slowly and clearly enunciated each of her words.

"I…ah, no, no. Of course not. It isn't a bother at all," Becky lied. "Are you all set to get going for our walk?"

"Oh, sure! But let me check my bag into a rental locker and we can be on our way."

"Oh, Sam, there are no rental lockers at this train station. Why not just lock up your suitcase in the trunk of my car? I'm parked right outside. And what the hell, it'll save you a few bucks."

Samantha smiled at her but it was a strange, almost condescending grin. She paused, and then shifted her eyes back and forth as if in a state of indecision. It was then that Becky peeked over her sunglasses and noticed the color of Sam's eyes. They were a deep emerald green. The color of her irises was so vivid that the eyes seemed almost like they were artificial.

"Oh, you're so sweet! No, I'll just put my suitcase in the checked baggage area. Then it'll be all set before I board the afternoon train to Boston."

Becky sensed that for some reason, Sam was uncomfortable with the suitcase situation.

She watched as the Midwestern high school student checked her baggage. She stepped away with her computer-printed ticket which she dropped into her army-green, canvas bag hanging from her shoulder.

"Okay, Becky, before we begin touring the campus, I thought we'd get some coffee and a bite to eat. It's my treat for you coming out here to meet me. I insist."

Becky noticed the small chip in her incisor tooth when Sam smiled.

"Huh? Oh sure! Let's walk up Chapel Street toward the Old Campus quadrangle. It's the Yale dorm where all of the incoming freshmen stay for their first year. There's a great place called Claire's where all the students go for coffee and good eats."

The sun was now warming up the air, and Becky opened up her jacket as the two girls strutted along the sidewalk. They chatted as they walked while the city seemed to come alive. People had come out early on this Saturday to enjoy the pleasant weather. Yale University students strolled around, grabbing coffee or poking into the boutique stores along the city-campus street.

"You know, if there's one place I'd like to see, it's the Yale Drama School. I've researched the celebrities who have attended there over the years—legends like Vincent Price, Paul Newman, Meryl Streep, Barbra Streisand, and so many more! I just have to see that! I really want to get into acting if…you know…even if college doesn't work out."

Becky got the message. *The girl with green hair who acts out each of her words wants to be in Hollywood.*

They stopped at an intersection and waited for the walk signal to light up.

"That's cool!" Becky said. "The Drama School is just up the street from here on Chapel Street. So, have you done any community projects yet?" *I won't mention I already read her bio about her life in Evansville. I think I want her to do more speaking than me. She already knows a ton about me!*

"Oh, yeah. I've performed in many plays. I prefer character acting for now, but soon will look for lead roles soon. I intend on joining a Drama Club my first day in college and hang with other theatre students. I really can relate to that group of kids."

"Hmm. Sounds like you really like it," Becky said, performing her own bit of acting—as if she were interested.

"Acting is fun but do you want to know something? I love all of it. I enjoy putting on the make-up and the challenge to morph into different characters with accents, dialects, and physical expression. I can disguise myself so nobody knows it's me; not even my grandparents. I love the wigs, the face grease, costumes, and all that shit. I've played an eighty-year-old woman, a plain-Jane nymphomaniac school teacher, and a French sailor in some of my town's repertory theatre plays."

"Wow! That covers a wide range!"

"Yeah. I especially liked being a young sailor in love with a singer from Paris. Don't get me wrong. I'm not gay, but it was fun playing a male for a change. I had to really work my voice for that gig, but the audience loved it!"

Becky was struck by Samantha's over-the-top passion and energy for theatre. She noticed how she spoke with her hands constantly in rhythm with her animated facial expressions.

Is she always like this, or is it a defense because she might be hiding something? Maybe she's just nerves, like Mom said. Whatever the heck it is, it's wearing. I've only been with her ten minutes and I'm already getting tired listening to her.

They entered Claire's, a boutique eatery that for decades had been popular with students and faculty members. They found an empty, small table next to the store-front window. Samantha dropped her shoulder bag onto the floor beside her chair.

After the waitress took their orders, Sam picked up again with the conversation.

"Okay, now I already know just a little about you, Becky, but please tell me more. I'm so interested in other people, especially kids from other parts of the country. I know something about your mom and a little about your dad, but now I want to learn about you."

Becky thought the conversation had taken a very strange turn. She decided she'd play it close to the vest when speaking with this girl whom she had just met.

"Oh, there's really not too much to me. I'm an honor student, like you, and enjoy all of my school subjects, especially in the Social Studies area. I…ah, play the flute in the high school band and…"

"And what about a boyfriend? You must have a boyfriend," Sam once again interrupted.

Becky grinned behind her dark aviator glasses which she had neglected to take off inside the cafe.

"Oh, yeah. His name's Jake. We met last year and have been going together for six months now."

"Six months, wow! That sounds serious," Sam commented with a lurid grin.

"Yeah, well you might get to meet him before you leave New Haven today. He might stop by to see us."

The grin melted and a more serious expression took over Samantha's face. "Oh, yeah, that would be cool."

The waitress brought their orders as Sam continued her interrogation.

"So Becky, tell me, what's it like being the only child? I mean, were you always spoiled? Do you like being solo or do you ever wish you had siblings?"

The question was a little too personal for Becky. It once again elevated her anger level. She stared at the girl from Indiana and began to fire back.

"It's nice. I never thought much about it. You've done quite the detective snooping, haven't you? Not just about me, but about my mother and father."

Becky knew she sounded defensive, but she didn't care. It was meant to be.

"Oh, it's not like I was spying on you, Becky. I was just really interested in your mother's career as a trial lawyer and…her desire for theatre acting. I found an article on the *New York Times* archived website. The story was about when she retired from her courtroom career. Her law firm was celebrating a big financial win, and your mom got briefly interviewed on her background."

The anger was percolating inside Becky now and she didn't feel like using her breathing routine.

I'm not going to let it go this time. In sports, the best defense is a good offense. So, I'm taking over this bullshit with my own attack.

"By the way, Sam, I read that you have a younger brother. What's he like?"

The green-haired girl hesitated before answering, seeming to sense the adversarial tone in Becky's voice, but when she spoke, she maintained her theatrical devices.

"Huh? Oh, ah…he's like most young brothers, you know, always playing sports and stuff like that."

"Really? What's his favorite sport?" Becky asked quickly.

An awkward tension now hovered over the tiny table between the two teenagers. Sam looked away as she answered the question.

"Oh, he's really into ah…basketball. Yeah, in fact, he's the captain of his school basketball team."

"And I read that you lived on a big wheat and soy farm with your grandparents. What's that like?"

"Oh, the truth is my grandfather sold the farm a couple of months ago. It…it was getting too much for them. In fact, a big-time developer bought the property. It will become a mini-mall in our tiny village outside Evansville." She paused. "Becky, I…."

It was Becky's turn to steal a play from Samantha's playbook—interrupting her before she could finish her sentence.

"So…what about your eyes, Sam? They look incredibly green. Are they naturally that color or are you wearing contact lenses?"

The probing personal question seemed to catch Samantha off guard, but she shrugged it off with a laugh and a sip of her coffee. It was time for the unique Midwestern girl to concede. It was becoming apparent Sam had met her match in the art of probing interrogation; jab for jab.

"Oh, yeah. I'm always changing the color of my eyes. I use those 'OTC' contacts. I have several pairs. I love to match them up with the current color of my hair. You should see my purple hair with purple contact lenses, really sexy and mysterious." She laughed out loud once again, attracting attention from the other nearby patrons.

"And your skin tone, Sam. It's got a great color. I take it you've been out in the sun."

The green-haired girl looked directly over to Becky, her smile morphing into a serious expression.

"It's a good tanning cream. I use it on stage and sometimes outside."

"Oh."

"And so, Becky Bing, how about we now do a tit for tat? You've had those cool, dark shades on since I met you at the station. What's the color of your eyes?"

Becky grinned at the strange and awkward interaction taking place. The two girls had just met and were playing some type of weird 'head game' inside the coffee shop. Without answering she reached up with both hands and slowly slipped off her aviator sunglasses. Staring directly at Samantha, she managed a fake smile showing her bright, white teeth.

Samantha looked into those eyes but didn't return the beaming smile. Instead a look of shock washed over the actor's face.

And what happened next was the last thing Becky would ever have expected.

CHAPTER FOUR

The blood in Samantha Rawlings' face immediately drained as she peered into Becky's eyes, now revealed after she'd removed her dark sunglasses. Speechless, Sam's mouth dropped open as she pushed her chair away from the table, distancing herself from her new Connecticut acquaintance.

"Hey, Sam, what the hell's wrong? Are...are you all right? Are you feeling sick?" Becky asked.

But there was only silence as the green-haired teen tried to regain some composure. She cleared her throat before speaking. The theatrical animation was missing.

"I...I just didn't expect...I mean, I didn't know..."

"What? What didn't you know, Sam?"

Samantha had to take in a deep breath, exhaling before she spoke.

"You're...you're Asian. I mean, you know, what...what are you, Chinese?"

Becky had no response. Suddenly all of the air seemed to have been sucked out of the coffee shop. The sounds from the other patrons echoed as if in a weird dream. Confusion, anger, and discomfort all swirled around the small table at once. She tried to control her emotions, breathing in and out before answering.

"What the hell kind of a question is that?" Becky responded loudly.

For the moment she had no regard of others hearing her loud and acrid question.

Samantha began to stammer.

"I…I…Oh, shit. I'm…I'm sorry, Becky. I…I…just didn't expect you to be…to be Chinese."

Becky stared across the table at the strange-looking specimen; her green hair with frosted highlights and costume green eyes. Her pale skin camouflaged as suntanned with some creamy substance. The army boots and olive-colored handbag made this girl seem like she was in several time-warped eras all at once.

But Becky had to let it go. Samantha was a negative presence who needed to be kept far away. Becky began her trained routine to regain balance, self-control, and discipline.

Take silent, deep breaths. Take them up from the base of my stomach. Exhale and count slowly to ten.

Becky did this for a while and felt herself letting go of the negativity.

The long and awkward silence was broken, not with words, but with a text message alert on Becky's cell.

It was from Jake. Becky lowered her head to read the message.

Just finished working with my mom. Where can I meet up with you two?

Without raising her head, she responded quickly. Her fast fingertips tapped a reply.

Drive to the New Haven Green for now. Not sure of our plans yet. Text me when you get in town and I'll let you know what we r doing.

After Becky raised her head, Samantha spoke to her in a low voice.

"Look, Becky, this is my freakin' bad all the way. I was just so…so stunned to see your face when you took off your shades. I mean, I had seen your mom's photo on the net with those courtroom articles. She's described as blonde and blue-eyed. I guess I stupidly expected you to look something like her, not the blonde part but maybe the All-American look. And, I thought the name Bing was very American. You know, like the fruit, Bing cherries. I just wasn't anticipating that you'd be…Chinese."

Becky stared coldly across the small table.

"I'm Chinese-American," she responded.

But she could tell from Sam's expression that her mind was now somewhere else.

The green-haired girl leaned over to reach inside her green canvas bag on the floor beside her. With Sam's head bent down below the table, Becky spotted a thin, white surgical scar line on the nape of her neck. The pencil-thin scar, nearly four inches in length, had tiny dots from surgical sutures on either side. It appeared to be from a cervical spine surgery.

Suddenly, Sam popped back up with a disturbed expression.

"Oh, this pisses me off! I couldn't recharge my phone on the train. I have to make an important phone call. I was supposed to let my grandparents know I was okay after I reached Connecticut. But now my cell's out of juice. Hey, can I please use your cell to make a quick call?"

Becky paused for a moment, considering the request after such offensive treatment. She slid her cell across the table. Samantha grabbed it and stood up.

"I'll…ah, do this just outside. Be back in a minute!"

The taller girl from Indiana quickly stepped outside through Claire's doorway, her fingertips tapping the cell phone.

Becky could still watch her through the large café window. Pacing back and forth along the Chapel Street sidewalk, the green-haired girl still had a perplexed expression while she spoke. Her free arm flailed in the air at one point and her voice became louder, but Becky couldn't make out the words, nor did she want to listen.

A few moments later, Sam returned inside and quietly handed Becky's phone back to her.

"Oh, thanks, Becky. But listen. I…I have to change my plans on the Yale campus tour. That phone call just got me a little rattled and I think I need to be alone right now. I…I need some time right now. I'm heading back to the station now and jumping on the next train up to Boston."

Surprised and relieved at the same time, Becky simply replied, "That's cool."

Samantha paid the check at the counter and the two retraced their steps walking down Chapel Street toward the station.

Becky texted Jake as they walked along the sidewalk in silence.

Meet me at NH train station now. Something came up. Sam's leaving for Boston.

Within a minute, Jake acknowledged the text.

Samantha broke the silence with another apology as they once again waited for the walk signal at the city intersection.

"I'm sorry about all this shit, Becky. Really I am, and…and I don't have a good explanation for you. The truth is I'm going through some personal problems right now. My stopping by here in Connecticut really wasn't such a good idea. Please, please accept my apology for the way I behaved."

Still waiting for the crosswalk light to change, Samantha reached into her canvas shoulder bag. She pulled out a package of cigarettes, Parliament Lights. Fingering one, she flicked a lighter she'd pulled from her pants pocket.

"Bad habit, you know," Becky commented without a smile.

"Yeah, I know. I only smoke when I'm stressed out."

Becky finally responded to the earlier request.

"Apology accepted, Sam. But when we meet again up in Boston, I might be less tolerant of this crazy bullshit and your racist attitude."

The light changed for them to cross the busy street.

"It isn't being racist at all, Becky. Believe me, I'm not like that! It was just a surprise that I didn't freakin' handle very well. It has nothing to do with you or you being Asian. When you took off your glasses I expected someone to look you know, a little like your mom but with black hair."

Becky zipped her mouth to let her thoughts take over.

It's freakin' done! There's no need to tell this racist bitch that my father is Chinese-American. That would really screw up her perverted assumption that the Bing family is lily-white. And I'd never tell her how I was adopted from Shanghai when I was a baby. She could never handle all of that. Besides, this chick doesn't need to know another thing about me or my family.

"Well, let's just hope we have better times up in Boston!" Becky finally said.

Sam simply nodded in quiet agreement as they stepped through the revolving door to enter New Haven's train station.

After claiming her suitcase at the baggage area, Sam stepped slowly back toward Becky.

"I'm sorry how this all turned out. I…I have a lot of things going on in my life back home and everything is kinda screwed up right now. It's personal and I think it's affecting me emotionally. I may return home soon. Who knows, I might leave before the end of the hoopla in Boston this week."

Before Becky could comment she saw Jake step through the station entrance.

"Oh, there's Jake," she said, waving her hand for her boyfriend to see.

When Jake approached, Becky introduced him to Samantha Rawlings.

"Hi, Samantha! Nice to meet you!"

But while the two shook hands, Becky focused on Samantha's expression. She noticed how the girl seemed in awe of meeting Jake, a mixed-race young man with darker-colored skin.

"Ah…nice…nice to meet you, Jake!" Samantha managed to respond weakly. "You know, you two guys are really cool. I mean it. You two have something going on here. Hey, I…I really gotta get going. I want to board the train early to get a good seat!"

"Well, it's too bad you can't stay, Sam, but I understand," replied Becky.

Jake reached out for the suitcase next to Samantha and lifted it up from the lobby floor.

"Here, Sam, let me take your bag to the boarding platform," he said politely.

"No! Ah…no thanks, Jake. I can take it," she responded with a raised voice, quickly grabbing her suitcase back from him.

"Well, let's at least walk you over to the door to the tracks," said Becky.

The three teens ambled over to the entrance leading to the outbound train platforms, Samantha now pulling her wheeled suitcase behind her.

Jake stopped and made a request.

"Hey, I'd like a photo of you two scholarship winners since I won't be up there in Boston. Let me take a shot of you guys before Sam leaves," he proposed. He quickly pulled out his BlackBerry from his jeans pocket.

"I…ah…I look a mess, really," Sam replied.

"C'mon, Sam, let him do it," Becky said, pulling at Sam's vest to get the two of them closer. "It'll make him happy. He loves taking pictures."

Jake slowly stepped back about six paces to get the two of them in his cell-camera screen. He then raised his cell phone with outstretched arms.

"Now, get a little closer together. Okay, now, how about some smiles, ladies?" Jake said, looking into the tiny screen and holding the device steady.

But before he could press the camera button, a man came rushing up from behind. His athletic build wasn't concealed under the light brown leather jacket and tight-fitting blue jeans.

The stranger collided into Jake with a tremendous jolt. The BlackBerry flew out of his hands and straight up into the air. But with his quick reflexes, he reacted, catching the cell phone mid-air before it fell to the marble floor.

"What the fuuh…," Jake yelled out.

"Hey, I'm sorry, buddy," the man said, still moving away. "I gotta make the next train. I'm runnin' late. Sorry!"

Before the man turned to jog away, Jake focused on him. His trim build was topped with a light blue baseball cap with a navy-colored letter "C" on it. The cap was low on his head with the visor nearly down to his dark sunglasses. His faded blue jeans topped black athletic shoes. The only noticeable features were a reddish-brown day's growth of beard on his face and a gold ring in his right ear.

After Jake composed himself, he looked toward the door where Becky and Sam had been posing. But only Becky remained there now. She stepped toward him. He stepped toward her.

"Geez, are you all right, Jake?" Becky asked.

"Yeah, that stupid bastard wasn't looking where he was running, I guess. I'm sorry I missed taking your picture. Hey, did Sam already leave?"

"Yeah. She didn't seem to want her photo taken anyway. She just told me she was anxious to get on the train, turned, and was gone."

"Oh, that's too bad. She seemed like a nice kid but…quirky."

"That's a word I hadn't thought of for her. Why do you say she was quirky?"

"Oh, it was just that suitcase thing. She didn't want me to pull it. The truth is it was light as a feather. I don't think she had packed anything inside of it."

"Jake! She had to have things inside. We're staying up in Boston for a week!"

"I'm telling you, it was as light as a feather."

Becky only stared up at him with a puzzled face as they left the busy train station. Walking towards Jake's car, she began to describe the encounter with Samantha Rawlings.

Jake started his older Honda Accord and pulled out onto Church Street.

"Hey, I think it's a great day for the shore," she suggested. "It won't be crowded along the seawall, but will still be nice there today. We'll come back for my car later."

"Cool," Jake replied, and accelerated from the intersection.

Becky continued to tell her boyfriend of the unnerving experience with the girl from Evansville.

"So, I don't get it. This girl calls you out of the blue and wants to meet with you in a big way. She's interested in you escorting her around Yale's campus, but then spends only twenty minutes with you and leaves. What the hell's with that?"

"I'm telling you, Jake, something happened back in the coffee shop when she discovered I was Chinese. But she didn't realize it 'til I took off my sunglasses. I mean, there's no denying it. Besides being obnoxious, peppering me with invasive personal questions, she's a freakin' racist! Man, was she shocked to learn I was Asian!"

Jake slowly turned his head to look over at his girlfriend sitting in the passenger seat. He reached over for her smaller hand and enveloped it inside his own.

"Geez, racial prejudice. That must be something just awful," he said, not hiding a smirk.

She playfully poked him in the ribs as he sat behind the steering wheel.

"I mean it, Jake. Everything was cool up until she saw my eyes!"

"Hmm. I believe you, Beck, but it really makes no sense. I mean, this chick is supposed to be intelligent and hopefully has an open mind. And, I'm sure there are Chinese people out there in Evansville, Indiana, so why was she so shook up?"

"I have to admit I was really pissed at her reaction to me, but in addition to that, she seemed just plain weird. I mean, I can accept green hair if that's her thing, but she seemed, I don't know…disconnected in some way."

"Disconnected?"

"Yeah. I thought she wanted me to show her around Yale's campus, yet she was convinced she'll attend Northwestern. She got the scholarship to pursue a degree in Social Studies, but theatre and acting are her real passion. And she asks a lot of questions but doesn't share too much about herself."

Jake pulled his sedan off the highway exit and headed toward the Connecticut shoreline facing Long Island Sound.

"Well, you'll be spending a few days with her up in Boston. Maybe you'll get answers to those questions while you're up there. "

They got out of the car and stepped toward the seawall. They sat upon the hip-high, cement barrier to enjoy the beautiful September afternoon. She then held Jake's hand and squeezed it affectionately.

"Yeah, you're right. I'll learn more about the mystery girl up in Boston, but…the question is…do I want to?"

CHAPTER FIVE

After spending time sitting arm in arm on the seawall, and talking with intermittent light kisses, they went for a long walk on the sandy beach with Becky still venting about her morning with the green-haired teen from Indiana.

Later, they decided to get something to eat. Jake drove to a nearby seafood restaurant, popular with the natives. They took a private table in the back corner of the eatery. She ordered fried shrimp; Jake, a clam platter.

"So, we can make this our six month anniversary dinner, a little early," Jake chuckled.

"I'm going to miss not seeing you in school. Not to mention at our jobs in the store every day."

"Me, too. But you'll be back next Friday. It'll go by fast. I'm anxious to hear how you liked touring Harvard and hanging out around that campus. Hey, there's a good chance you'll be living up there next year."

There was silence as they looked at each other. There was no need to speak about the anticipated anguish of being separated the following August.

"First, I have to get accepted. What about you? Any word from NYU or Carnegie Mellon?"

"Acceptance letters come out next month for early admissions," Jake said and looked away somewhat sheepishly.

"What's wrong?" Becky asked.

"There's something else I've been holding back from you. I also applied to one other school that I haven't told you about. I wrestled with the decision to apply but decided to go ahead with it. I haven't even told my mom about applying to this other school."

Becky's eyes grew wide with anticipation. She knew Jake with his intelligence and school grades could be accepted into almost any school he wanted.

"I bet it's Harvard, isn't it? You want to live closer to me up in Cambridge, right? Or…or is it MIT, still up there in the same neighborhood? C'mon, Jake, tell me. Where did you apply?"

He looked at her, reached across the table, and squeezed her hand a little tighter with a heartfelt smile.

"Believe me, Beck, I'd love to be close with you for the next four years. But no, it's not Harvard or MIT."

"Then what school is it?"

"It's where I came from and where my dad worked. It's the Air Force Academy in Colorado Springs."

A long silence hung in the air. The waitress brought their lunch orders then left the table.

"Oh. Your father would have been so proud if you went to the academy, Jake."

"I know. And that's why I did it. Last Tuesday was the second anniversary of his death in Afghanistan. I told you how he loved the academy so much and how I liked living in that atmosphere. I got a nice recommendation from Senator Sadowski. A Congressional recommendation is a requirement for admission to any military school. I mailed the admission application package a few months ago."

"So if you get it, you'll be going back to your hometown, Colorado Springs."

He nodded silently. They both began eating with no more talk. The quiet between them was something that rarely happened.

Towards the end of the meal, Jake stared into Becky's eyes.

"Beck, I think my mom is ready to move back to Colorado. My aunt doesn't need her help anymore here in Connecticut. Mom really misses her friends in the Sierra Club back home."

Becky wasn't ready for this conversation. She'd just had a negative experience with some weird racist girl, and now her boyfriend was looking for approval to move on.

"I know you'll be accepted, Jake. With your background and being the son of a deceased Air Force combat hero who used to teach at the academy, it's certain you'll get in. And I also know how your mom loves hiking in the mountains with her friends in that club."

"I know that. But I'm so torn. I really like you and we're really best friends, but if we continue in this relationship, it would have to be long distance."

Becky's hand reacted, reaching across the table to gently massage his smooth, dark skin.

"And prolong the inevitable between us?"

"Maybe. I can't take up any of your time, your life, if it will end within months. And you may have opportunities to meet other guys."

He put his head down.

"Jake. You know my mantra. Live in the moment and don't worry about the past because it's already gone, and never worry about the future because it hasn't yet come. So for now, let's enjoy the present time. Let's just enjoy each other for today."

After leaving the restaurant they returned to the beach, now busier with the inviting and warm autumn afternoon. Couples, families, and runners brought energy to the breezy shoreline facing Long Island Sound.

Jake surprised Becky when he opened his car's trunk and pulled out two kites. Each had a colorful dragon face and a long ribbon-bowed tail. They kicked off their shoes and ran along the soft, sandy beach, this time with strings held tightly in their hands. Soon their bright-colored kites were airborne, sailing and swirling in the sea breeze. They laughed and ran around barefoot in the sand until the sun began its descent in the western sky.

There was no further discussion about their relationship.

* * *

When Becky returned home, she told her mom and dad the visit with Sam Rawlings had been uneventful. She wanted to avoid any discussion of the distasteful encounter. Instead she switched topics to talk about the fun she had with Jake at the beach, flying kites.

That evening, while Becky placed the dishes into the washer, she asked her father a question. Since it was after six in the evening, she stuck to their routine language learning habit and spoke Mandarin.

"Dad, do you know what's wrong with our studies at school?"

"爸爸，你知道学校的研究有什麼错吗？"

"Ba ba, nǐ zhīdào xuéxiào de yánjiū yǒu shéme cuò ma?

"What?"

"Shénme?"

"什麼？"

"We study all the easy education topics; history, science, and math but we ignore the more difficult topics."

"我們学習容易的课题: 如歷史，　科學和數學,但我們却忽略了更困難的課題."

"Wǒmen xuéxí róngyì de kètí: Rú lìshǐ, kēxué hé shùxué, dàn wǒmen què hūlüèle gèng kùnnán de kètí."

"More difficult topics? Like what?"

"更困難的課題？是什麼?"

"Gèng kùnnán de yìtí? shì shénme?"

"Human topics. For example, prejudice and racial discrimination are problems. We talk about it, but we really don't resolve it."

"人類的主題.　例如，偏见和種族歧视的问题。我們谈論它，但我們卻不解决."

"Rénlèi de zhǔtí. Lìrú, piānjiàn hé zhǒngzú qíshì de wèntí. Wǒmen tán lùn tā, dàn wǒmen què bù jiějué."

Her father paused while preparing a pot of tea.

"You are correct! Prejudice and discrimination is everywhere. Often is it painful to face the truth."

"你是正確的！偏見和歧視是無處不在.　往往是痛苦的面對事實."

"Nǐ shì zhèngquè de! Piānjiàn hé qíshì shì wú chù bùzài. Wǎngwǎng shì tòngkǔ de jiějué."

Later, Becky packed for her trip to Boston. It was nearly midnight when she slipped into her bed. A sudden chill ran down her spine just as she pulled the covers up to her chin.

That must just be the excitement of the week ahead, she thought. *Or…is it an omen of something that's in store for me?*

* * *

"Welcome to Boston and the Copley Hotel, Miss Bing! We hope you have a great stay heaah, and if you caahn't find something you need, please ahhsk!"

The young registration clerk had an Irish appearance with fiery, red hair, bright blue eyes and a warm smile. The Boston accent with the broad A pronunciations completed the handsome man.

"Heaah is your key caaahd and this is yaaw room numbaah." He pointed to the digits 1775 written on the card holder.

"Thanks. I will!" She returned his friendly grin and smiled at the irony of getting room number 1775, the year of the legendary Paul Revere ride and start of the American Revolutionary War in this very city.

She took the elevator to the 17th floor and marched along the carpeted corridor toward room 1775.

After dropping her suitcase on the room floor, she immediately stepped over to the large hotel room window to look out at the view.

Her room was high enough so she could see the John Hancock building with its blue-green glass color. Further in the distance was the historic icon building, The Customs House, with its unique tower, visible in the foreground to the Boston Harbor. She focused on the deep-blue harbor and its many shipping docks. She mused that one of those wharves was where Paul Revere, Sam Adams, and his Sons of Liberty revolutionaries had dumped crates of tea into the harbor in protest to tariffs imposed by King George III of England.

She then turned her attention to a glimpse of the white church tower in the famous North End section of the city. It was the legendary Old North Church from where the critical lanterns warned of the British soldiers' approach—"one if by land, two if by sea."

The scenery brought everything together for Becky—her research paper gaining her a prestigious college scholarship, the Boston accents kept from colonial times, and now the spire of the historic church.

After putting away her clothes she opened a small gift basket. Inside were some healthy snacks, fruit, a Boston map, and a package addressed to her. It was a welcome package for all the scholarship winners, including a schedule with information of the week's activities, and some tourist brochures.

A simple card instructed each attendee to be at the Abigail Adams Room at six o'clock sharp. An informal buffet dinner was scheduled to kick off the annual program and provide a chance for event facilitators and other students to meet and mingle.

Becky lay down on the hotel bed to stretch out after the three hour drive from Connecticut. Just as she closed her eyes for a nap, her cell alerted her that she had a text. It was from Jake.

Beck, call me when you're settled in.

But before she tapped in the number, there was a knock on her door. She went to the door and looked through the peephole. A young man was standing at her door. He had a close-buzzed start to a goatee that appeared only days old. The rest of his face was clean-shaven.

"Yes, who is it?

"I'm Drew Lane, a facilitator with the Scholarship Program. I just wanted to know if everything is all right."

Becky opened the door wide to face the man.

"Ah, sure. I just got in but I think everything's fine."

"No, it's not!" he replied in a stern tone.

"Huh? What…what's wrong?"

"This!" He pushed open her room door and took one step forward.

"Hey, what are you doing?" Becky yelled out.

He immediately stopped at one foot inside the room with one hand propping open the door.

"I'm showing you what you did wrong! Do you realize what I could have done to you and your belongings within minutes?"

"Huh, I ah…."

"Look, Becky. One of my responsibilities with the annual program is Security. That means making sure each student acts with caution while staying here at the hotel in the city. You should never have opened the door for me."

"But you told me you were…"

"I could tell you anything. You didn't ask for any identification through the peephole. You just assumed I was truthful and opened the door. Now, will you promise me you'll never do this again while you're here in the hotel?"

"I…ah, sure. It was stupid. I should have thought about that."

"Not stupid, but dangerously naïve. And just to let you know, I'm doing this to each and every student here on the floor. You're not the only one. Now, I will see you and the others at six downstairs. Enjoy the program. And, if you have any issues about security, let me know!"

Becky stared at the intense man. She focused on his square-jawed face with his dark, hazel eyes and cleft chin. He turned and stepped briskly out into the hotel corridor, slamming the door behind him.

CHAPTER SIX

Becky stepped into the Abigail Adams Room just before six. There were several students and some adults milling about in the attractively decorated room with impressive glass chandeliers. Just inside the doorway sat a female Copley Hotel employee at a table draped in a linen tablecloth.

"Hello! Can I have your name, please?"

"Oh, it's Bing. I'm Becky Bing."

"Welcome, Becky. Here's your name tag. Please pin it to your blouse. Just walk on in and get to know the others. The formal part of the program gets underway at six-thirty."

Becky kept her dimpled smile as she walked into room. She stepped up to the refreshment table which held appetizers, cold drinks, and juices. Her eyes panned the room looking for the mysterious high school scholar with the green hair. But she was nowhere in sight.

A tall young man with wavy, golden locks lowered his head to read her name tag. His voice had a distinctive southern drawl.

"Hi, Becky! I'm James Blackstone from Raleigh, North Carolina. How are you?"

She shook his extended hand.

"Oh, hi! I'm doing just fine. It's really nice here."

"Yeah, I like the hotel. Have you met anyone else yet?"

No need to explain Sam Rawlings now.

"Ah, not really any of the other students. But I did meet Mr. Drew Lane."

"Oh. Yeah, me too. I got my butt chewed by him about security. Did you?"

"Yep. I sure as hell learned my lesson!"

The two picked up soft drinks and filled their small china plates with a variety of appetizers. As they walked along the table, they both introduced themselves to other students reading each other's name tags.

Becky felt herself tensing up, awaiting a theatrical entrance from the mysterious green-haired girl who'd abruptly left her at the New Haven train station.

About a half hour later, the hotel door attendant walked among the crowd, quietly asking everyone to sit at the tables so the program could get underway.

A box formation of long tables enabled four students at three sides. This accommodated the students while the fourth side of the square was reserved for the head table made up for the program faculty.

Becky sat between James to her left and a boy from Michigan on her right, who she had just met. Her eyes panned around the tables once again. But Samantha Rawlings still had not joined the other scholar students.

Becky was also aware as the students took their seats that only eleven teens sat down. One chair was empty. She began reflecting.

So Samantha Rawlings really did have some personal problems. She wasn't just blowing me off! Maybe she changed plans and returned home to take care of other issues. If so, she'd be back in Evansville now. Sadly for her, she forfeited her scholarship money and the week in Boston.

A woman who appeared in her late thirties, dressed in a stunning, cranberry-colored dress accented with stylish gold earrings and necklace, stood up to welcome the students. Her youthful, curvy figure wasn't lost in the dress. Her attractive, raven-black hair cut in a short wavy style shined under the chandelier lights.

"Welcome, students, to this exciting American History Scholars Program! My name is Brooke Gleason. I'm a history professor at nearby Boston University where I earned my PhD in American Social Studies. I'll be a program facilitator for this wonderful event over the next few days. And we are so happy to be here with you!

"We have a lot to go over in this, our first dinner meeting, and you'll find that we want a relaxed atmosphere, where you ask questions whenever you have one. Tonight's informal buffet is an opportunity for all of us to get to know one another since we'll be together for the next few days.

"All of our conference sessions will be convened right here in this beautiful Abigail Adams room. Now, I want to introduce Dr. Helen Brisbane at my left. Helen is another professor of American History from Dartmouth University, and a prolific author of several history books. She too has written about many interesting facts that have been misrepresented in some of our history texts. I'm sure you'll enjoy meeting Helen, and talking to her about her teaching, her research, and of course, her popular books."

The tall African-American woman in her forties stood up. She wore a white knit dress that complimented her shiny white, pearl earrings.

"I look forward to meeting each of you over the next few days and discussing your college futures and beyond. But as Brooke said, tonight is an opportunity for all of us to get to know one another a little bit. And so, for this first meeting we have distributed a list of all twelve scholarship winners and their hometowns."

Becky quickly skimmed the list of attendees.

Brad Atkinson------------Santa Barbara, California
Becky Bing----------------North Haven, Connecticut
James Blackstone---------Raleigh, North Carolina
Brenda Cornwall---------Westchester, New York
Lynn Faulkner------------Santa Fe, New Mexico
Valia Mancito-------------Laredo, Texas
George Norris-------------Franklin, Michigan
Tran Nguyen--------------Cherry Hill, New Jersey
John Peterson-------------Salt Lake City, Utah
Samantha Rawlings------Evansville, Indiana
Frances Reese-------------Atlanta, Georgia
Jasmine Tariakas---------Billings, Montana

Dr. Brisbane sat down and Brooke Gleason continued with her message.

"And now, to my right is Mr. Drew Lane. Drew, who is a doctoral candidate from Columbia University, has joined us this year to facilitate the program. And he will wear many hats with us this week. He will act as our Security Officer and official tour guide for those who want custom tours of this beautiful and historical city, Boston, Massachusetts. You will get to know Drew who is a wealth of information about American History, the Revolutionary period, and of course his hometown of Boston."

Drew stood up while Brooke sat down. The handsome young man smiled and waved before speaking to the teenagers.

"I've already met each of you already. I gave you my only lecture of this week on safety and security and hope you all enjoy your stay. As I told you, if you need me for anything, just ask. I just finished my work in American History at Columbia and have returned home to finish my dissertation. But, as Brooke mentioned, I'm a native of this city, and have worked for Boston Tours in the past. I have been a guide and docent. In fact, that was my part-time job while an undergraduate and graduate student here in town.

I look forward to giving you all a personalized tour of this great and historical city. If any of you have any interest in a particular site, let me know and we can schedule a visit. But as Dr. Gleason just told you, I'm also responsible for everyone's security. You're all new to Boston and we ask that you use caution as you would in any large city. If there is anything suspect or that makes you feel uncomfortable, please let me know as soon as possible."

Brooke Gleason stood back up just as Drew sat down.

"Yes, and since almost all of you are eighteen years of age, you need not be chaperoned during your free time here in the capitol of Massachusetts."

A hand went up from one of the students.

"Yes, please give us your name before you ask your question."

The attractive girl stood up, showing her low scooped neckline boasting an ample cleavage. She had a curvy figure and dressed to show it off. Her makeup was well done but gave her a seductive, older look well beyond her age of eighteen.

"My name is Lynn Faulkner and I come from Santa Fe, New Mexico. I wanted to ask something. Ah, will we have a bedtime curfew while we're staying here this week?"

Some friendly chuckles came from the group.

"Oh, Lynn, I'm glad you brought that up. You may not know it yet, but all of your rooms are on the seventeenth floor, and we prefer that all students be inside their rooms by ten-thirty each evening. Now, are we going to check on that? No. Do we ask you to help us out on this policy? Yes. And to let you know, my room, Drew's and Helen's rooms, are all on the same seventeenth floor. But while there are all kinds of opportunities for free time and latitude as to where you go, we want all of you to be safe while you're here.

"So, Lynn, to answer your question, we don't intend on doing any bed-checks but sincerely hope you all cooperate with our request to avoid any problems."

"Thank you," Lynn responded politely before sitting down.

Brooke Gleason smiled then continued speaking.

"Now, before we go into the next administrative process, which involves filling out a brief form with your current cell phone numbers and other information, I did want to explain to all of you why we have one empty seat in the room."

Becky looked over at the empty seat on the other side of the square layout of tables. She anticipated the explanation to come.

She'll announce now how Samantha Rawlings changed her mind and headed back to Indiana to handle those mysterious personal problems. It'll be the same story she told me. She also left me at the station supposedly taking a train up here, but maybe she exchanged her ticket and took a train headed back home.

"The young lady who is supposed to be sitting in that chair called early this morning," Dr. Gleason explained. "She told me she had come down ill this past week. She's now recovering from a severe throat infection. She is coming along, but has no voice with some residual laryngitis. So, the good news is she intends to give it another day and will catch up with all of us here tomorrow."

Becky's face furled in puzzlement.

Crazy chick, Miss Rawlings, must have come down with one hell of a sudden infection. She was fine when she met with me yesterday in New Haven.

Dr. Gleason continued. "Before we go further, we've all just heard Lynn Faulkner introduce herself and where she came from. We want all of you to get to know the other scholars. This event is a once-in-a-lifetime experience. So when we next meet here tomorrow morning, and for subsequent sessions, we'd like each of you to sit beside someone whom you haven't been with before. And always wear your name tags.

Now, I think it's time we go around the room and introduce yourselves with your name, where you come from, and what your ambitions are in college." She pointed in the direction of a young man at the left table. "Let's start here."

The young man stood up. "My name's Tran Nguyen. I'm from central New Jersey, and I'm a second generation Vietnamese-American. I love this country and became intrigued with the Declaration of Independence and the Revolutionary War when I was in middle school. I want to teach high school Social Studies."

The introductions went around the box diagram of tables quickly. After Becky sat down, James stood up, followed by the last student, a girl dressed in a simple flowered-print dress. She was slow to rise up from her chair.

The young woman was medium height with granny-styled glasses. Her brunette hair was pulled back into a ponytail. Her dress contrasted to her pale complexion. She had no makeup or jewelry on her.

Becky leaned forward into the table and turned her head to look at the girl who slowly began speaking in a soft, timid voice.

"Hello. My name is Samantha Rawlings."

The name resonated in Becky's brain.

What? Did she say she is Samantha Rawlings? What the hell's going on here? This is crazy!

She grabbed the arms of her chair and froze like a statue.

"I come from Evansville, Indiana and I hope to follow in my grandmother's footsteps. She and my grandfather cared for me and my brother while she taught middle school. Her teaching career lasted over thirty years. And like her, I want to teach Social Studies at the middle or high school level."

She sat down. Her face had flushed a bright pink during her brief presentation.

Becky remained frozen in place, seated in her chair. She was numbed at what she'd just heard. Her mind raced. *What's going on here? Who the hell is this girl? She shouldn't be here. She's a freakin' imposter. I already met Samantha Rawlings and it isn't this girl. But...apparently, I'm the only one here who knows that.*

What happened to Samantha "Green Hair" Rawlings? I gotta check out the program to learn who really has the laryngitis.

Brooke Gleason thanked the group and went into a few more administrative issues before they all got up to the buffet tables just set up by the catering crew.

The students mingled more while selecting the meal items. But while everyone chatted at the tables, Becky's eyes kept shifting from the empty seat opposite her to the girl who'd said she was from Evansville.

I gotta get to this chick and find out what's with her. I'll wait 'til she goes up for dessert then join her at the buffet table.

While sipping her iced tea, she felt a sudden tap on her shoulder. The touch startled her. She quickly turned around to look straight into the hazel eyes of Drew Lane. He had crouched down to her eye level to talk to her.

"Hey, Becky. I just want to apologize for the way I shook you up earlier today. I didn't mean to intimidate you."

"Oh, I ah...it was okay, Mr. Lane. And, ah, I had it coming. I'll never open a hotel room door without knowing who is on the other side...for the rest of my life."

Mr. Lane grinned then uncoiled from the crouching position. "Okay. I've got lots to do upstairs. See you tomorrow!"

"Sure!"

When she turned around again, she noticed the other kids going up to get dessert.

"You gonna get some cake or pie, Becky?" James asked.

"Oh, ah, sure."

She looked around his back to the seat next to him for the timid girl. It was now empty.

"What…what happened to ah, that girl sitting beside you, Samantha?"

"Oh. She told me she wanted to get up to her room. I guess she didn't want any dessert. Man, she sure is a shy one. She seems nice though," James responded.

"Hey, you know what, James? I really don't have any room for dessert. And I have to give my folks a call back home. I think I'll just go up to my room now too. It was very nice meeting you."

"Oh, yeah, sure. See ya tomorrow!"

CHAPTER SEVEN

Becky stepped into the elevator accompanied by two senior citizen hotel guests. She pressed the button for the seventeenth floor. When she got off, she encountered nobody else on the floor as she walked briskly to room 1775.

Her first reaction after double locking her door was to call Jake. She tapped her cell with his number before flopping on the bed.

“Hey, so how’s it going up at Beantown?” Jake asked.

“Boston and this hotel are great so far, but I’ve encountered a bit of a weird mystery.”

She took a few moments to playback to her friend what had taken place at the buffet reception.

“My God, that’s freakin’ bizarre. I thought you and Sam would be hanging with the other kids tonight. Hey, I guess you were right. This green-haired girl is just some kind of a whack job.”

“But who is she? Was she some kind of imposter? I already met Samantha Rawlings and despite me not liking her, this plain-Jane girl and the green-haired actress are complete opposites.”

“You told me how Sam said in the coffee shop she had problems back home. Do you think she returned to Indiana?”

"I did at first, when I saw the empty chair. I figured she bailed out on the whole thing and just forfeited the scholarship money. But then this new girl stands up and tells the group she's Samantha from Evansville. She also told us how she was brought up by her grandparents and her grandmother was a former school teacher. Just like Green Hair told me."

"Hmm. Well, this plain-Jane could be the imposter. She could have read the same material in the student profiles. But this, this is really weird."

"And criminal!" Becky added. "It's against the law. It's fraud and stealing another identity for financial gain."

"But wait! Let's turn it around. What if 'Samantha Green Hair' didn't want to lose out on the scholarship money and really did have to return home for some personal emergency?"

"Huh?"

"What if she had hired and paid this girl or somehow persuaded her to take her place at the Scholars Program? This way, she'd meet the requirement by attending the event, of course by proxy, but she'd still collect the checks when she attends college."

"You think she prepped this timid girl to take her place and tell everyone she is Samantha Rawlings?"

"Yes, but just for the few days of the program up in Boston. You told me earlier there were no photographs of the scholarship winners in the program booklet, so who at the hotel program would know what the real Samantha Rawlings looked like? And after she checked in, nobody would ever know the difference."

"Boy, I'll say one thing. Sam sure picked a girl who's nothing like herself. I mean, this girl seems really shy and blushes very easily. Green Hair would have put on an entertaining, theatrical performance when she got up to introduce herself!"

"That reinforces how this girl's really nervous in her imposter assignment. It's a new role for her and she doesn't want to get caught or there could be criminal charges."

"I wonder where she comes from. Maybe she's a relative, like a cousin or perhaps some school friend," Becky mused.

"That's a possibility."

"And she probably comes from Evansville," she added, "because if she didn't, she could get tripped up with some probing questions from others who might know that area."

Becky flopped down on her back upon the large hotel bed. She stared up at the ceiling, thinking about Jake's theory. "Hmm. I think you might be right, but…"

"I know. You have to verify it. I know you all too well, Becky."

They both chuckled and switched topics, talking about nothing in particular. They whispered their affection for one another and how they hated to be away from each other. There was no more talk about breaking off the relationship.

Before switching the light off for the night, Becky walked over to the hotel room desk. She opened up the program pamphlet, thumbing immediately to the student profiles. It didn't take long to match up those students who'd attended the meeting. She jotted a check mark on each profile page. When done, she knew the name of the missing girl. *Brenda Cornwall is the student with the throat infection. It was Brenda who was supposed to be in that empty chair.*

The booklet paragraphs described Brenda coming from an affluent community of Westchester County, New York. Like the other eleven, she had excelled academically. She loved American History, but Brenda also had aspirations of becoming a professional singer during or after college. She had won many talent competitions with her singing from an early age.

Becky read each line of the student's bio carefully to learn more about the missing winner. Brenda had described her parents, noting as an only child she had lived a privileged childhood and wanted for nothing. She travelled extensively with her parents in Europe, South America, and Asia. She was quoted saying she had "a deep compassion for the less fortunate children around the world." She worked closely with her parents to make significant charitable donations and provide support to help those children who needed assistance.

Becky closed the booklet, turned off the bedside lamp, and pulled up the bedcovers. She breathed deeply and meditated for several minutes to turn off the stories running in her mind. Soon she was totally relaxed and fell into a deep sleep.

* * *

The radio-alarm buzzed loudly at six-thirty in room 1775.

Within minutes, Becky was dressed in running gear and out onto Copley Square, stretching her legs.

Although the hour was early, there were several other joggers already out, getting in their morning run before traffic built up in the city.

After her run, she saw housekeeping staff filling their carts before performing their duties. When she walked by the matronly lady in the hotel uniform of maroon and beige, she noticed she was Asian. Her name tag on her collar displayed the Chinese name, "Mei Yang."

She smiled at the older woman, and then spoke to her in Mandarin.

"How are you? My surname is Bing. First name is Becky."

“你怎么样？我的姓是冰。贝基是名.”

“Nǐ zěnme yàng? Wǒ de xìng shì bīng. Bèi jī shì míng.”

Upon hearing her native language, the housemaid beamed at Becky.

“I’m fine, thank you.”

“我很好。谢谢.”

“Wǒ hěn hǎo. Xiè xiè.”

Inside room 1775, Becky quickly showered then slipped on a pair of dark- green linen slacks topped with an open-necked, white, buttoned jersey over a flower-rimmed blouse collar.

She took the elevator down to the second floor meeting room for the breakfast buffet. On the elevator she chatted with John Peterson, an African-American student from Salt Lake City, Utah. They entered the Abigail Adams room together to see other students already stepping by the long and festive buffet table offering hot and cold breakfast items. The hungry students filled their plates. Instinctively, she turned around looking at the others as they approached the table.

But there was only one student who intrigued her now—the one using the name Samantha Rawlings. Just as Becky poured hot tea, the timid girl entered the room. She was alone.

Becky quickly stepped toward her, carrying her porcelain cup.

“Good morning, Sam! Hey, why don’t I save you a chair and we can sit together?”

“Huh? Oh, sure. Thanks, Becky.”

Within minutes, the quiet teen from Indiana joined Becky with a plate of scrambled eggs, a muffin, and orange juice.

“Thanks for asking me to join you, Becky.”

"Oh sure, Sam. We're all supposed to get to know one another, which I think is cool, so I thought I'd get to know you."

"Well, the first thing you'll learn is that I prefer being called Samantha rather than Sam. I actually hate that shortened name."

Becky stared at the plain-looking teen while recalling what she had been told on that first phone call with Samantha Green Hair.

"Oh, Becky, please call me Sam. I prefer it to Samantha. All my friends call me Sam."

"Oh, sure, of course, Samantha. That's, that's good to know. In your introduction, you mentioned you come from Evansville, Indiana. What's that like?"

"It's a lot different than here in the East. Besides, I grew up on a farm with my grandparents."

"That must be cool."

"I loved it, but my grandparents just sold the farm property this past spring. Those acres that once grew corn and soy will become a commercial development. It's really strange. My grandma and grandpa work so hard all of their lives, just getting by and then all of sudden, they must sell the farm to make ends meet."

"Hey, but that's cool. You'll still be a family living in Indiana!"

As the two ate breakfast, Becky offered a bit about herself, her ambitions, something about her mom and dad, and of course, her relationship with Jake.

"Say, I remember reading in your profile that you had a younger brother," Becky commented.

"Oh, yeah, his name is Glen," she responded while reaching for the salt shaker, but her hand hit her glass of milk, spilling it over the tablecloth.

"Damnit! I'm such a freakin' klutz. I'm always doing stuff like this. That's something else you should know about me, Becky."

The two girls mopped up the liquid with extra napkins and soon resumed their conversation.

"Now where were we? Oh, yeah, my brother, Glen. He's only fourteen but he's such a great kid! He loves his music and nature. The two of us always spend time outdoors when we can."

"I bet he also likes playing sports like baseball or basketball."

"Huh? Oh, no. Glen's not into any sports. In fact, he has no interest in following sports!"

Becky's mouth dropped open wide. She recalled what Green Hair had told her in New Haven. *"Oh, my brother's really into basketball. In fact, he's the captain of his school basketball team."*

"Oh, Glen doesn't play basketball?"

"No. No way!" Samantha replied.

The Scholarship Program facilitator, Brooke Gleason, suddenly came up behind the two girls with her warm smile. She alerted them that the morning program would begin shortly.

Becky excused herself to go to the ladies room.

She texted Jake out in the corridor:

Hey! This Samantha thing is getting weirder and weirder. Wish u were here! Will call u later. xxoo.

When she returned to her seat, Dr. Gleason was standing at the head table. She presented the day's agenda after all the student scholars were seated. She announced there would be free time in the afternoon for students to prepare their five-minute final presentation if they needed it, or to explore around the city sites nearby. As an alternative, she suggested they could arrange a private Boston tour of the famous Boston Freedom Trail with Mr. Lane.

"Oh, and I have some good news! Our twelfth winner, Brenda Cornwall, is driving down here from New York State. Her throat infection has improved but she still has some laryngitis. She'll join us here for tonight's dinner and hear Dr. Brisbane's interesting talk titled, 'Teaching the Real American History.' And I know all of you will find Helen's talk humorous and entertaining!"

The morning program proceeded with a brief video about the American History scholarship followed by a lively and comical talk from a visiting history professor from Wellesley College.

Lunch time came quickly along with another opportunity for the students to mingle and meet.

But Becky had only one student she now made her target. She caught up with Samantha once again and asked if she'd like to join her for a walk along the famous Charles River after lunch. The historic river was just three city blocks from the hotel.

"Sure, but let me first give my brother a quick call from my room. Then we can go!"

Becky met with others during lunch but kept an eye on the curious Samantha.

After returning to room 1775 and double-locking the door, she immediately called Jake.

CHAPTER EIGHT

"Hey Jake, how's work at the store going today?"

"Oh, I haven't started my shift yet. It's boring being here without you. Hey, your last text intrigued me. What's going on?"

Becky talked non-stop, bringing Jake up to date on the two Samanthas and how characteristically different the two girls were.

"She wants to be called 'Samantha' while Green Hair told me she always preferred 'Sam.' And listen to this. Her little brother hates sports and isn't the captain of the basketball team as I was told in New Haven. In fact, he has no interest in sports."

"Hmm. Seems like we have to find out who is the imposter, and who is the real Samantha Rawlings."

"But how? Green Hair isn't anywhere to be seen."

"What else did this Samantha tell you?"

"She told me her grandparents had to sell their family farm."

"And was that back in Evansville, Indiana?"

"Yep! She said it was a big deal in the local village; the farm had been in the family for generations."

"Well, I can look into that bit of news and verify it while you're up there in Beantown. That story might tell us something about the family. What we really need is a snapshot of the real Samantha."

A thought flashed across Becky's mind at the suggestion.

"Look, I'm going out for a walk with her now and will find out more. But wait, I'm thumbing through the program pamphlet. I found her bio page. She attends Granby High School. Oh, and she told me she sang in the school choir. Can you look that up? Maybe the school's got some photos online. Then I can tell if she's an imposter or not."

As the two girls walked toward the banks of the Charles on the pleasant September afternoon, Becky attempted to learn more about the shy girl from Indiana. She sensed this plain-looking student was honest and humble—nothing like the girl she'd met in New Haven.

But is she the real Samantha Rawlings? Or is she some paid imposter?

The Charles River provided a perfect venue to watch the energy and activities on either river bank; the Boston side and the Cambridge side.

They watched the colorful college rowing teams moving their long, sleek shells swiftly by in perfect cadence. Bleached white sails contrasted with the dark, blue water tacking back and forth along the serpentine river. Joggers, runners and walkers paced along the river way under the shadows of the historical colonial town and its eclectic mix of old and new buildings.

The two chatted informally at first, but along the return walk, Becky asked her first probing question.

"So, have you decided on which school you're going to attend?"

The girl chuckled. "Well, I can only afford local, in-state schools. So I applied and will probably go to Indiana U. Which of course, I'm still happy about since I won't be too far from my brother and grandparents. I'm so happy I was one of the winners of the scholarship. It'll really help. I'm also getting some other financial awards from local groups."

"Hmm. How about other interests? I play the flute in my high school marching band and love all sports, especially golf. How about you?"

"Not much, really. After school I spend time with my brother, Glen."

"Oh, so you never had interest in, say, something like acting or performing on stage?"

Samantha laughed loudly. "You gotta be kidding! I'd die of stage-fright. But why did you ask about acting? Is that another one of your interests?"

They reached the wider sidewalks of the Boston streets approaching the hotel. But something caught Becky's attention.

The *click, click* sound of high heels striking the cement echoed behind them. As they continued at a moderate pace, Becky quickly turned her head briefly to see a young, slender, blonde dressed in a navy-blue business suit and white blouse walking behind them. She had on a stylish, light trench coat, unbelted and opened. A black handbag hung from her shoulder. The rhythmic clicking came from shiny stiletto heels. Most of her face was hidden behind her shiny, golden blonde bangs and oversized, dark sunglasses.

The woman kept pace with the teens, following about ten yards behind. The traffic light changed at the popular Copley Square, allowing pedestrians to cross the busy Boylston Street. When they walked toward the Boston Public Library, Becky stopped and faced her new friend.

"Samantha, do you have your driver's license?"

"Yeah, sure, I do."

"Can I take a look it?"

She paused staring back. "Becky, you ask a lot of freakin' questions. I almost feel like you're some kind of reporter or investigator or something. Do you always ask people so many personal questions when you're just getting to know them? It really is annoying!"

Before she answered, she looked beyond Samantha, seeing the blonde once again, clicking past them. The woman now held a cell phone to one ear but no words could be overheard.

"Samantha. I'm, I'm sorry. No. I never ask this many questions of someone I just met. But…I have to tell you something. It's important but I'd rather tell you privately—either up in your hotel room or mine."

The answer seemed to startle Samantha. She leaned backward, away from Becky. Her voice now had a decidedly anxious tone. She pulled out her driver's license from Indiana, flashing it in front of Becky.

"Look!"

The photo ID issued by the state of Indiana verified that this young girl standing before Becky was the real Samantha Rawlings from Evansville, Indiana.

"What…what is it, Becky? What the hell is it that you can't say to me here that has to be so…so private?"

Becky paused before looking into her peer's inquisitive eyes.

"I, ah, had a visit from a girl on her way up here to the conference. She asked to meet me at the New Haven station."

"And what happened? Did you meet her?"

"Yeah. I sure did but she only stayed a while and it was bizarre and awkward. We had coffee. Then she told me she wanted to leave and continue up here to the awards week program. She left on a train around noontime. I told her I would catch up with her up here. But she never showed up."

"Really? Well, who was…what was this girl's name?"

Becky looked directly into her new friend's eyes and paused before answering.

"Listen. She told me she was Samantha Rawlings and that she came from Evansville, Indiana."

The pale-skinned girl's mouth dropped, not hiding her shock at hearing the revelation.

"What…what? What the fuuu…." She stopped mid-word with a look that pierced Becky's eyes. "Let's go up to my room. It's room 1770!"

Becky hesitated before jogging to catch up with her companion.

Oh my God! What am I getting myself into here? Should I go into her room alone? What if she is an imposter with a fake Indiana ID? What if she's just acting surprised? Is she going to do something to me since I may have now called her bluff? Or, is she really who she says she is? I wonder if anyone else is with her. I guess I'll find out once I get inside room 1770.

CHAPTER NINE

Becky and Samantha followed the heel clicking blonde with the trench coat into the Copley. Before turning to the bank of elevators, the strikingly well-dressed woman turned to catch a glimpse of the teens not far behind her.

The blonde quickly headed straight into the nearby hotel lobby lounge, Periwinkle's, noted for its generous drinks and local seafood raw bar.

Without a word, the two teens stepped from the elevator and marched along the seventeenth floor corridor to Samantha's room. As they crossed the entrance threshold, Samantha hit the wall switch. Becky slowly closed the door.

"Okay. Now tell me about this…this bitch you met who used my name," Samantha said as she sat down on the edge of the bed.

Becky pulled out the desk chair, turned it to face her, and sat down. While she spoke, she looked directly into Samantha's eyes to try to detect any nervousness.

She continued her story of what had happened back in Connecticut the weekend before the program began. She left out no details of the bizarre mystery. "So, that's why I asked you so many questions, Sam, ah…Samantha."

"But, why…"

A text alert came in from Jake on Becky's iPhone.

"Excuse me for a minute," she said to Samantha.

Becky looked at what had come in from Connecticut. It was a photo of Samantha's younger brother, Glen Rawlings, taken from an Evansville, Indiana news story. It told how the fourteen-year-old overcame several handicaps to play the violin. It was especially poignant and uplifting since Glen was wheelchair bound. Becky looked at Samantha.

"I have one more question, but not about you. Why doesn't your little brother play sports? You told me he had no interest in any sports."

"Huh? Oh see, he's unable to play anything athletic. He was born with a severe physical handicap and…."

Becky stopped her mid-sentence, holding up her iPhone with the photo.

"I think he's cute. And tell Glen I'd love to play a duet with him someday; his violin and my flute."

Samantha took the cell device and smiled without any comment.

"So you knew?"

"My boyfriend just sent it to me. I had asked him to find out who the real Samantha was and to do some research. Now I definitely know I'm talking to the real one!"

"I have no idea who that green-haired girl was. But I gotta tell you it scares the shit out of me. Why would anyone want to impersonate me with you?"

Becky retold the part of the story when Green Hair had been astonished to learn her new friend from Connecticut was Chinese.

"That just doesn't make any sense. What does she have against Asians? I don't know anyone who would do this and…steal my identity. And then she doesn't show up here. Becky, I…or we…should report this."

"Yeah, but what the hell do we report? And who do we tell? It's just some weird chick with green-colored hair who met me, using your name. Nothing illegal has been done as far as we know. And her prank, or whatever, is now history…no pun intended."

Samantha chuckled, then got up from the bed and paced around the hotel room.

"I suppose you're right. And I really don't want to bring police into this. The last thing I want to do is make my grandparents nervous. But I wonder if we should tell some of the scholarship leaders."

"Hey, it's getting late. Did you sign up for Drew Lane's tour of Boston?"

"Yeah, I did. But first I just have to call home. I'll come to your room in about fifteen minutes."

Becky returned to room 1775 and called Jake.

"Hey, thanks for the pic of Glen Rawlings!"

"Does it help you determine if this girl is legit?"

She explained what had taken place in Samantha's room.

"At least I know who I'm with up here. We both can't figure out why some whack-job would pull a prank like that! It just doesn't make sense. There was no money involved, so what the heck was the point to the whole thing? It wasn't funny as a joke, and it served no purpose other than pissing me off."

"Well, it's all behind you now, so go out and enjoy your tour of Boston with Samantha."

Minutes later, the two girls walked side by side down the long corridor. As they turned the corner headed toward the bank of elevators, they came across a housekeeping cart. It wasn't Mei Yang working today, but a younger, thin woman who was grabbing supplies to bring into the adjacent room.

The two girls walked on either side of the cart. But Samantha didn't notice as her shoulder bag accidentally snagged the black, plastic trash bag hanging on the housekeeping cart. As she walked by she pulled the trash bag with her, spilling the contents on the corridor floor.

"Oh, shit! There I go, doing it again! What a klutz! I'm…I'm so sorry," she told the thin hotel staffer.

"It's okay. It was an accident," the employee said.

"Here, let me help clean up this mess I made," Samantha said.

Becky retraced her steps to help out. As the housekeeper picked up the large, spilled bag, a few more discarded contents fell out. But one item in particular caught the attention of both teenagers.

Becky's heart stopped beating as her eyes became riveted on the manufactured hairy item. She froze, staring at the wig lying on the carpeted floor. Its bright green color was hard to miss.

"Oh, you two run along, I can get this," the housekeeper politely told the girls as she picked up the discarded hairpiece.

"Wait! Can I take a look at that wig?" Becky asked.

"Huh? Oh sure. It was probably someone dressing up in a crazy party outfit. Let me tell you kids, we see lots of weird stuff from our guests."

Becky's hand reached out. Her fingertips touched the shiny, synthetic material. She turned it over in her hand. The lifelike wig was cut in the standard bob-styled fashion. The hair fibers were a mix of neon green and frosted white. It was identical to the hair she had seen last weekend in New Haven.

The housekeeper took the wig from Becky's hand.

"Hey, you shouldn't be touching that thing! See, I always wear latex-gloves when I clean and handle trash," the woman said, displaying her transparent rubber gloves.

"Geez. I never hear about green-colored hair and now it's come up twice in one day! What do you think about that, Becky?"

Becky stared down at the fabricated hair piece.

"It's the same one, Samantha. At least I'm pretty sure this is the same wig that crazy chick wore when we met last Saturday morning."

"Huh? You mean it wasn't really her natural hair, dyed green? You're telling me it was fake?"

"To be honest, I didn't even think about whether it was her own hair dyed green or if she was wearing a wig."

Becky turned to face the hotel staffer.

"Miss, do you know where this came from? I mean, do you remember which room had this wig in the trash can?"

"Sweetie, I just empty the garbage from the room trash buckets. I learned to never look inside; for my own sanity. I haven't a clue where this hideous wig came from. What an ugly color!"

"But which rooms have you cleaned so far?"

The slender woman reached for a clipboard hanging on her cart and handed it to Becky.

"Ah…here! Here's my room list. All the ones I cleaned so far are on the seventeenth floor."

Becky peered down at the clipboard. It held a preprinted form listing the rooms to be cleaned for the day. Those already cleaned had a box checked off. She thought quickly then pulled out her iPhone from her small shoulder bag. She positioned the clipboard and took a picture of the form with the cell device. She then turned to the housekeeper.

"Thank you, Miss. I really appreciate this. It's just that we want to learn who might have worn this wig."

"Okay, but I gotta get going. I'm behind on my routine."

The girls headed for the elevator, taking the car down to the hotel lobby.

During the descent, Becky texted Jake with an update. But it was Samantha's concern that made her feel uncomfortable.

"Holy shit, Becky! If…if that's the same wig that was worn back in New Haven, it means that girl you met who impersonated me is staying in this hotel."

"Yeah, I'm thinking the same thing. She must be here at the Copley."

"My God! This crap is just getting too damn weird. I wonder if this…whoever she is signed into the hotel using my name at the registration desk."

"Maybe we can check that out. But we have to learn first where that green wig came from and we must do that soon!"

Becky noticed Samantha's color was draining. A worried expression froze on her face.

"Hey, look, don't worry about this. It'll be all right!" Becky said.

"I'm going to report this bullshit incident. I have to report it!"

"Look, we're going on Drew's tour of Boston, and we better hurry. After that, let's meet with him privately. He's the security guy for the program. As far as we know, this is a Scholars Program issue and not a Boston police case."

"Not a police case—yet," Samantha responded.

There were seven students gathered around Drew in the hotel lobby standing in a semi-circle. The other five, unencumbered with mysteries, who Becky and Samantha now joined, were excited to begin the walking tour of Boston.

"Now, I'm going to lead you on the standard 'Freedom Trail' tour. It's only three miles long and doesn't take long to walk. Before we begin the tour, I want you all to know that I grew up here in Boston, and worked as a tour guide during summers when I was an undergraduate. It helped me pay my tuition and I learned more than what is told to visitors on the tours, but I'll get to that later. Now, let's get going!"

They began at the central green park of the city, known as The Boston Common. It was the same area once used for cattle grazing, artillery training, and hanging witches.

The tour was interesting to the young American History buffs and Drew proved to be informative and entertaining. He showed his humorous side during his colorful anecdotes and posed for pictures with the students along the famous Freedom Trail of Boston. When they reached the Old North Church in the North End section of Boston, Becky asked her new friend, James, to take a picture next to the handsome tour guide, Drew Lane.

“Now, you all know about Paul Revere, a patriot, Revolution leader, and famous for warning the colonists that the British soldiers were starting the famous war. But you all know it wasn’t he who hung the lanterns in the church tower. It was the parish sexton, Robert Newman.

-Since you’re a special group, I want to give you a private look into the Old North Church. There are many nooks and crannies in this landmark church and I used to lead tour groups through each of these doors, except for one that is off limits.”

It was clear to the students that Drew was in his element giving the tour. His youthful appearance, outgoing personality, and knowledge of the area made for a delightful experience for all of them.

“Except one door? That’s intriguing. What’s behind that one door, Drew?” James asked.

“You’ll see soon, my friend, you’ll see soon,” he responded. A devilish grin curled his lips as his eyes looked into the faces of his seven teenaged followers.

CHAPTER TEN

The sun had begun its descent in the western sky as the group entered into the Old North Church main doors. Drew acknowledged the guard with a personal handshake and greeting.

"Good to see you again, Drew. It's been a while," the older man said, then smiled at the teens as they marched by into the beautiful, colonial-styled place of worship.

The interior pristine pews, painted in a glossy white and partitioned, were overshadowed by the balcony that hung overhead. Drew led them throughout the historical church pointing out everything from the architecture to the unique bust of George Washington, considered by experts to be the best likeness of the Revolutionary War General and first president of the United States.

"Okay, guys, now go ahead of me and spend a few minutes looking at things on your own. In a little while, I'll have a surprise for you," Drew said.

The students fanned out with their cameras, taking photos of artifacts that interested them. But Becky's curiosity got the best of her as to what their leader was up to with his surprise. At an oblique angle to their tour guide, she watched as Drew stepped over to the side of the church's sanctuary. He stopped in front of a small altar table placed against the back wall. Drew panned around to ensure the students were busy before his hands reached out in front of him.

Becky looked away but quickly turned to see him open a drawer, pull out a key ring, and slip it into his jeans, before closing the desk drawer.

Drew walked off briskly from the altar and stood in front of the first pew.

"Okay, guys, are you ready now to see the most interesting part of this Old North Church?"

"Sure, what is it, an old hook where Paul Revere hung his tri-cornered hat?" asked James, getting a few giggles from the crowd.

"Nope! This is something much, much more interesting." Drew's voice then playfully changed and took on a macabre, creepy tone. "Follow me, my friends, as we step down into the dark and nasty underground of this centuries-old building. I'll show you something that most groups never get to see in the forgotten cellar of the Old North Church."

The students formed a single file line as Drew led them into a narrow hallway. At the end was another wooden door. They watched as their leader withdrew a key ring from his jeans pocket. He singled out one key, inserted it into the door-lock, and opened the door, stepping across the threshold. After he did so, he turned once again to face his youthful followers.

The group of teenagers stepped anxiously down into a dark and colder area. Drew turned a light switch on but the dim-wattage, naked bulb didn't illuminate much of the stone and brick cellar alleyway ahead of them. After getting deeper into the cobwebbed and musty-smelling corridor, the leader reached up and grabbed a flashlight hidden on top of an old wooden beam.

The light beam from the hand-held device played against the corridor walls. Soon they reached the area of crypts containing hundreds of skeletons. The students became solemnly quiet as they walked by. Each took time to read the scripted text on the outside of the crypts written hundreds of years ago.

"These...these are dead bodies down here," Samantha spoke out so that everyone could hear her. There was a noticeable nervousness in her voice.

"Yeah, pretty cool, eh?" Lynn Faulkner commented.

"That's right. Many people are buried in these walls and some crypts are just filled with the remains, ah...bones of some people who have no names. There are skeletons all around us," Drew said with a playful smirk on his face.

Drew explained the history of the underground crypts that over the years had held over 1100 skeletons. He explained how the burial service was a significant revenue producer for the church.

"Anyone think it's creepy down here in this dusty, dirty cellar?"

"It's not just a cellar," James replied. "It's a freakin' underground graveyard!"

The teen group all spoke softly echoing James' statement. They each looked around at the underpinnings of the famous structure. The heating ducts, water pipes, and wiring showed how the building had been updated many times since it was originally built in 1723.

Drew told the scholar students how the notoriety of the Boston church all but obscured its official name, Christ Church, after the Revolutionary War.

"But now, I have the *piece de resistance* of this historical underground tomb. But we must go through just one more door. Follow me."

The students muttered and giggled to one another that they might be in for something creepier than the skeleton crypts. A few were nervous about what they might come upon next.

Drew waited until the group of seven came closer to him. The door had an official sign on it in decal letters.

KEEP OUT
ABSOLUTELY NO ADMITTANCE!
The Christ Church Board of Trustees.

"Now, I'll open the door and we'll peek inside."

The students huddled closer, some clutching each other, preparing to take a peek. Drew turned the handle, and with a theatrical motion, swung the door wide open.

"Voila!"

The students reacted to what they saw with quiet shock.

"C'mon. Let's go inside." Drew led them into a room that was fitted up into an apartment kitchen. Bright white walls and floor cabinets surrounded a sink, a microwave oven, and kitchen stove. The cream-colored Formica counter held a toaster, a modern electric can-opener, and other sundries.

The hidden apartment was so misplaced in such a dark, dingy church basement.

"Walk around; there's more to this place. It's bigger than you might think."

The students next stepped into what appeared to be a small living room, replete with flat screen TV, a studio couch, and a small upholstered chair. Off to the side was a modern tiled bathroom with a stand-up shower. Adjacent to that was a neatly decorated bedroom with a king-sized bed a full-sized closet and bureau.

"Okay, Drew. This is a surprise. You're not going to tell us this is the renovated apartment where Paul Revere slept on those nights his wife kicked him out of the house," Becky said with a smile.

The students laughed loudly at the witty remark.

"No, it wasn't Paul Revere who stayed here, but it was someone you know."

The students yelled out names of people they thought might be the mysterious resident of the underground apartment.

"Sam Adams?" one student shouted.

"I know, I know, John Hancock!" another offered.

"What about the sexton who put the lanterns up in the steeple of the church. You know, one if by land, two if by sea. Oh…what was his name, ah, I know, Robert Newman?" James asked confidently.

Drew laughed at the attempted answers.

"Nope! You're all wrong—but all are good guesses! The man who built and actually lived in this underground pad was none other than the man you're looking at right now!"

"Huh?" many voices said.

"I told you I worked as a docent here for Boston Tours part-time and during the summers. Well, there came a time when I had no place to live. Without a family and not wanting to sponge off of others, I made a proposal to the Church trustees. It was a fair deal. I would build an apartment down here and become the live-in night watchman for the church. I did that through my college years including the time spent working on my Master's degree in American History. It wasn't until a year ago, that I couldn't do it any longer since I had to spend more time at Columbia University working on my doctorate. But I still have access to my old pad that comes in handy, especially now."

"Oh, man, that is such a cool story, Drew," said James in his slow, North Carolina drawl.

"But wasn't it, you know, kinda creepy, being alone down here at night with all these scary skeletons next to your little apartment?" Samantha asked.

"Naw. I just talked to them when I walked by and they always left me alone!"

"Hey, Drew, do we get to go up into the church steeple and see where those lanterns were shown to let Paul Revere know the British were coming?"

"Of course, I'll bring you all up there soon. But keep in mind two things. The lanterns only burned for about a minute or less. If Newman kept them burning for a longer time, the soldiers, who camped out all around these streets, would have seen them also. So Newman would be telling them something was going down in old Beantown. They would know that their secret attack was no longer a secret."

"And what's the second thing, Drew?" Becky asked.

"Well, this is no surprise to you, Becky, since I read your full research paper, but the others, like most people, always refer to the Redcoats as the British. True, they came from England and were British, but—so were the colonists including Sam Adams' Sons of Liberty and the rag-tag group of Revolutionaries. The colonists who lived here referred to themselves as British, because they too, were natives of England."

"So what did the colonists call the British soldiers?" Samantha asked.

"Well, most people referred to them as 'Regulars.' That meant they were members of Great Britain's Regular Army. Or, sometimes they just called them—Redcoats."

"So, the famous expression—the British are coming, the British are coming! —was never spoken, even though it's quoted in a lot of books and other places," James chimed in.

"You're absolutely correct, James," Becky added. "That expression was made up by someone who was a good marketer or promoter. It was probably a poster or T-shirt vendor!"

The students broke out in laughter until Drew spoke again.

"Okay, guys, we got to leave from down here and head back up the stairs. I'll meet you all in the church sanctuary and we'll climb up inside the steeple. From there we'll head back to the hotel."

CHAPTER ELEVEN

The students became energized with the personal tour of Boston's Freedom Trail from Boston Common to the Old North Church. They buzzed about Drew Lane being an excellent tour guide. Becky and Samantha dawdled in the hotel lobby, inspecting the fine gifts in the Copley boutique.

"I have to say, it's nice to have someone as knowledgeable as Drew in our Scholars Program. I like how he really knows what he's talking about," Becky said.

"Yeah, and it sure as hell doesn't hurt that he's so hot-looking!" Samantha interjected.

Inside the lobby of the hotel, Samantha stopped short.

"What is it?" Becky asked.

"Oh, I just remembered I need to stop by the hotel store and pick up something. I'll meet up with you later at dinner tonight."

Becky got off at the seventeenth floor and walked briskly down the long corridor. As she turned a corner, she saw a woman wearing dark sunglasses entering a hotel room. She saw Becky approaching. The woman then quickly did an about face and went inside the room, closing the door behind her.

Becky slowed, recognizing the woman as the same blonde who'd clicked behind her and Samantha, and then later stepped into the hotel bar, Periwinkle's. When Becky walked by the door, she noticed the room number. It was 1792.

Later that evening, the scholars assembled for light appetizers and soft drinks before dinner was announced at the formation of tables covered with mint-green linens. The chatting was more lively and relaxed since the students were more familiar with their peers.

When the program leaders and students were seated just prior to the evening meal and presentation, all eyes were riveted onto one person. She sat in the seat that had been empty since the first evening of the American History Scholarship program.

Dr. Brooke Gleason, wearing an attractive, multi-colored dress and gold pendant, stood up to welcome the students. The colors complimented her jet-black hair and again accented her fit figure.

"I'm so happy that we're now at full occupancy. I want you all to welcome Brenda Cornwall who has just joined us."

The group followed Gleason with polite applause. The program leader then resumed speaking.

"As I mentioned to you, Brenda has bravely driven here from Westchester, New York. Because she's still resting her voice from the viral infection, she will not be speaking to anyone tonight and will take each session one at a time. Her doctor has confirmed she is not contagious and can do everything with us but must not speak until her throat is completely healed. This is a real personal blow to Brenda because you may have read in the program biographies that she's an accomplished singer. She has already performed at the Met in New York City. So, we must all be patient and hope her voice returns soon."

Becky stared at the girl sitting at a right angle from where she sat at the table this evening. The girl with brunette-colored hair styled in a closely-cropped, almost buzz-cut style smiled but didn't look at the group of students. She wore dark-rimmed glasses with yellow-tinted lenses. These contrasted with her milky-white complexion. Her crimson blouse with scalloped-neck matched the deep-red color of her eye-shadow. When she smiled, her mouth reflected shiny, silver braces covering her teeth.

Becky then focused on the boy sitting to Brenda's left. It was Tran Nguyen, the Vietnamese-American from New Jersey. He appeared to talk with Brenda almost non-stop, pausing only for the quiet girl to nod her head to him as a silent form of agreement. She also noticed Brenda had a pad of paper to communicate with Tran, jotting down words every so often so he could read her comments.

Becky's eyes shifted back to the head table as Dr. Brooke Gleason continued.

"Now there's one item left I must announce as our salads are being served. As we discussed at our first session, Drew Lane is here as one of our program facilitators but let me again remind you, he's also responsible for security issues while you are here. If there's anything that troubles you, or makes you uncomfortable during the Scholarship program, please contact Drew as soon as possible."

Drew stood up to segue from Dr. Gleason's repeated preamble. All eyes were riveted on the handsome young man. His auburn, trimmed goatee was coming in more thickly, adding some distinction to his youthful face.

"The reason Brooke has made this reminder is important. We already have had a minor security incident occur. I'm happy to say it was brought to my attention and it was quickly resolved. So please follow Dr. Gleason's advice and come see me if anything is not in order while you're here at the Copley and the Scholars Program."

As Drew sat back down, Samantha's eyes quickly found Becky's stare. They both were thinking about the mysterious imposter who they referred to as simply "Green Hair." There was no sense going to the police now. If it ever came to them reporting the bizarre twist of events, they would go to Drew.

There was a brief intermission after dinner and prior to the history talk presented by Dr. Helen Brisbane. Becky took the opportunity to approach Brenda and introduce herself. As she did so, Brenda held out a very limp hand and shook Becky's. Her smile was filled with metal as she stood back from Becky as though she might be contagious.

"Hey, I guess you guys had a great tour today, huh?" Tran asked. His voice, high pitched and friendly, matched his feminine body language.

"Yeah, it was interesting, Tran. Too bad you didn't join us," Becky answered.

"I know. But I'm too much into art so I visited the museum and popped into the Massachusetts College of Art. It was impressive. Tomorrow I'm going to the famous Berklee College of Music. And that's why Brenda and I've been chatting, or should I say…I chat, she jots. I play the cello and of course Brenda is a terrific singer, so we're both interested in music."

Becky excused herself as the speaker stepped up to the podium, arranging her notes. But before leaving to take her seat, Becky saw Brenda bend down to replace her notepad into her handbag. Tran courteously waited for her. Out in the hallway Becky read a new text from Jake. He wanted her to call him when she was free.

After Dr. Brisbane's entertaining talk, the group dispersed. Some went back outside to enjoy the warm September evening. Becky waited for Samantha to catch up with her on their way up to the seventeenth floor.

"So, do we go to Drew now with our story? I mean, I'm willing to let it go, but finding that green wig in the trash just creeps the hell out of me," said Samantha.

"I know, but listen. I can't be totally sure it was the same one. Those wigs are sold in costume shops everywhere. And, like the cleaning lady said, it might have been some hotel guest costume party or a party prank. So, I'm willing to let it go, if you are."

"Hey, that reminds me. We'll never know for sure which room the wig came from, but your iPhone has the list of rooms the housekeeper already had cleaned. Which rooms were they?"

"Good point!"

Becky pulled out her cell device and brought up the saved photo of the cleaning woman's clipboard. She talked while she scrolled down the photo.

"Here, let's see, she had checked off each room she already cleaned. Oh, look, she had only finished with three rooms. And they are 1790, 1792, and 1793. That narrows it down, but I'm still not sure it will help us. Besides, those room guests may have already checked out by now."

"Not really, Beck. Remember what Dr. Gleason told us on the first evening? The seventeenth floor has a block of rooms just for people involved with this scholarship event."

"Hmm, you're right," Becky said as she suddenly became pensive. "Then who the hell is that blonde who I saw going into room 1792?"

"What are you talking about?"

"I saw a blonde, in fact, the same one who walked behind us the other day at Copley Square. She was opening the door to room 1792 then stepped inside."

"That's weird. But she might be a friend or guest of one of the faculty people running this program. You know, like some of the speakers, or Dr. Gleason, or Dr. Brisbane who spoke tonight."

"Or…she might be an overnight guest of our tour guide and cute security guy, Drew Lane," Becky proposed. "The thing is we still don't know who registered into Room 1792."

"Yeah, and the people at the front desk will never tell us. That's confidential."

"Damn, I hope that blonde wasn't in Drew's room. I was saving that hottie for me!" Samantha said with a girlish grin.

They both laughed before saying goodnight and heading off to their separate rooms.

While Becky got ready for bed, she called her parents and told them all about the Boston tour, the evening's presentation, and the friends she had met. Because of the evening hour, she spoke Mandarin with her father.

"I really like this city, Dad!"

"我真的很喜欢这个城市，爸爸！"

"Wǒ zhēn de hěn xǐhuan zhège chéngshì, bà ba!"

The two chatted for a while. Her father expressed his excitement for his daughter's first trip away from home on her own.

She then switched to English when her mother got on the line. Purposely, she didn't mention the mystery of Green Hair, but her mother asked a direct question.

"So, tell me, Sweetie, how are you and that Sam Rawlings getting along?"

There was a long pause. Since Becky was so close to her mom, lying was never an option. But she answered nimbly to avoid any details.

"Oh, we're getting along just fine, Mom. But I mix it up with all the other kids. They're really nice and very interesting."

After concluding the phone conversation with her folks, Becky called Jake.

The two spent a few moments whispering how they missed each other.

"So, are all you scholars having fun and getting along?" Jake asked.

"Of course!" Becky told him about the dinner talk given by Dr. Brisbane, and the fun tour of the Old North Church. She talked about some of the other friends she had met, telling him how the twelfth scholar student, Brenda Cornwall from Westchester, New York, had just joined them.

"So this Drew guy is a History doctoral candidate and your local tour guide. That's pretty cool."

"Yeah, and he's only in his late twenties. The girls all think he's hot!"

"Oh, yeah? And what about you? Do you think he's hot?"

"Me? No, of course not!" Becky replied with a giggle.

"Hey, you know something? If this Brenda Cornwall, who just joined your group, is related to the Cornwall family from upper New York State, you're mingling with a very wealthy student!"

"Really?"

"Yeah. That family is well known for their charity work and financial support for underprivileged children. They are written up in the *New York Times* quite a bit. They're always noted for their philanthropy. I think the family's known for making their wealth in the oil transport shipping lines."

"Hmm. I read about that in her bio piece. Her appearance is misleading. She has very short hair, thick tinted glasses, and dental braces. Oh, and she uses lots of make-up. Right now, she's nursing some throat infection and still has laryngitis. She can't speak with us to save her voice. I guess she's an accomplished singer and performed once at the Met in New York City."

"Hmm. So, what's up for your group tomorrow?"

"We get to tour any of the college campuses here in town. Did you know that there are seventy colleges in the greater Boston area?"

"It must be a fun city! There's gotta be college kids everywhere you look. You'll love it, Beck; if Harvard accepts you there. And I know it will."

"I hope so. I now want to come to school up here more than ever before!"

Quiet lingered for a few moments, before Jake changed topics.

"Hey, I did a little more research online for the Rawlings family from their suburb of Evansville, Indiana. I found a story on their little village newspaper."

"Anything interesting?" she asked.

"The sale of the Rawlings farm was a big deal for the neighbors. That farm had been sort of a historical landmark in the community for many generations."

"Yeah, Samantha told me it was in the family for a long time."

"I still couldn't find any photo of Samantha. Are you sure she's not a paid imposter, so the real Samantha Green Hair can collect the scholarship money?"

"Jake, I can't be sure, but my gut tells me she's the real deal. Since we found the green wig, she's worried sick that she or both of us are being stalked inside the hotel. I'm not worried about this Samantha."

"Holy crap! That's just too damn weird, Beck! Do you think that crazy racist chick is somewhere in your hotel? I hate to think she might be there spying on you."

A pause hung in the air while she absorbed this.

"Hmm. Well, I have no idea why I'd be stalked, and Samantha has no idea why Green Hair tried to steal her identity. I told her the green wig could be a coincidence, you know, just to relax her a bit, maybe me, too.

"Well, it wouldn't surprise me if it was the same wig. You know, she told you she had experience as a stage actress. You told me she liked putting on stage make-up, and costumes which includes wigs. So, she'd know where to get good costumes and how to put on a well-made wig."

Becky and Jake continued talking when the loud ringing of the hotel desk phone startled her. She asked him to hold while she took the call, anticipating a wrong number.

But it wasn't a wrong number. Samantha's shy voice was on the line.

"Hey, Becky, I'm sorry to bother you. I just can't sleep, still thinking about all that's going on. If you're up for it, do you want to join me downstairs in the hotel coffee shop? We can get a cup of tea or a shake of something. I just need to relax a little before going to bed."

"Ah, sure. I'll come by in a few minutes."

Becky finished her call with Jake. She reflected how the tone of the dialogue was different now between them. There was an unspoken understanding their relationship wasn't going to advance beyond what it was. But she was still grateful that she and Jake would continue to talk with one another after they were off to their respective colleges. They'd always be friends.

Becky and Samantha took an empty elevator down to the lobby. Within minutes, they were seated in the restaurant booth and had ordered two of Boston's famous ice-cream "frappes."

"Thanks for doing this, Becky. I just can't fall asleep this early tonight. My mind keeps spinning with what you and I are involved with here."

"It's fine. I wasn't that tired either."

A voice addressed them, forcing them to turn their heads.

"Hey guys, mind if I sit for a minute with you? I just ordered some take-out for my room, but I have to wait a bit."

The voice belonged to Lynn Faulkner, now dressed in blue jeans and an oversized navy blue sweatshirt with *New Mexico State* printed on it in large letters.

"Of course not, Lynn," Becky answered.

Lynn slid into the booth's bench seat next to Samantha. "I'm playing it low-key tonight after all the excitement last night!"

"What? What excitement was that?" Samantha asked.

"Oh, I figured it would all have been out in the 'rumor-loop' by now. It's what Drew Lane referred to tonight about that 'security incident" that he said was resolved."

"Yeah, I remember. No, I…ah, we haven't heard anything about that," Becky commented.

"Well, it was about me. The incident happened late last night outside of my hotel room door."

Both girls leaned in.

"Oh no! What happened, Lynn?" Becky asked.

"It was totally my fault. I did something I shouldn't have and I'm so thankful that my hero, Mr. Drew Lane, came to my rescue."

"Huh?" Becky said.

Lynn looked around before answering.

"Look, I came here with a phony ID. It's a brand new fake New Mexico Driver's license. I just got it a few days before I left home and flew into Boston. My girlfriends have been daring me to try it out in a city bar. So, I figured if I'm gonna try it, I might as well use it far away from home in case I got caught. And I thought this is about as far away from home as I can be."

"Oh, no! Did they arrest you?" Samantha asked.

"No, that's not it! I had no problem getting served. I went into that club across the street. Without acting nervous, I looked straight ahead and climbed up on a bar stool. Then I ordered a draft beer. The bartender asked for my ID. I casually pulled out the phony driver's license and gave it to him. He had no problem with it. Within a minute, I was sipping a glass of Sam Adams and feeling pretty damn proud!"

"You did? Then what happened?" Samantha asked, curious and excited.

"I sat at the bar, but decided to drink the beer quickly, because I was alone and suddenly sensed a lot of eyes staring at me. I finished the beer, paid for my drink, left a tip, then swiveled off the bar stool and walked back over here to the hotel."

"Then what happened?"

"I waited for the elevator, which quickly became full with other guests returning to their rooms. I looked around and didn't want to breathe heavily with the smell of alcohol in my system. I was the first to get off at our seventeenth floor. I went to my room door, swiped my card key, and went in feeling gloriously successful. I couldn't wait to call my friends!"

"So, where was this so-called security incident Drew spoke about?" Becky asked.

"Well, as I'm on the phone talking to my best friend back home, there's a tapping on the door. I check the security peep hole and didn't recognize the man. He was older, about forty years old, and had a serious look on his face."

"Oh, no! It was an undercover cop, right?" Samantha asked.

"The man called me by name. He said, 'Lynn, open the door. I have to talk to you right away. It's important.'"

"When I asked who he was he just repeated what he told me. But I noticed he was looking side to side then he put his head down. I guessed someone had come up to the floor because I heard the sound of a room door handle being turned."

"Oh, my God! Who the hell was this guy?" Becky asked.

"I stared through the security lens and remembered seeing him at the bar. He had come into the elevator right after me. In any case, I yelled out loud for him to go away when Drew came onto the scene. Luckily, Drew's room is across the hall from mine. He was entering his room and became suspicious of the guy knocking on my door."

"What happened?" asked Samantha.

"Drew introduced himself to the stalker, and then there were some words I couldn't hear. Drew escorted him down to the hotel security office. I found out later the bastard was an ex-con who was just out of jail on parole. He had been in the bar earlier where I got served the beer. Evidently, he followed me back to the hotel without me knowing it."

"Oh my God! What was he in jail for?" Becky asked.

"He had been convicted for multiple sexual assaults!"

"Holy shit! Do you know how lucky you are?" Samantha asked.

"Well, yeah. I'm so 'f-in' lucky Drew came to my rescue!"

"What do you think will happen to the ex-con?" Becky asked.

"Not much. He'll be tried for breaking parole, drinking in a bar, and will go back behind bars. But I sure as hell learned my lesson! I told Drew the whole story and then gladly turned over my phony ID to him to destroy."

"So you were the 'security incident' huh?" Samantha asked.

Just then one of the restaurant staff brought over Lynn's take-out in a white paper bag.

“Okay, guys, I gotta run. I have calls to make before I turn in.”

“Hey, Lynn, before you leave, I have a question. You said Drew’s room is across the hall from yours. What’s the number of his room?”

“Oh, ah, it’s number 1792.”

“Room 1792!” Samantha parroted.

Becky looked across the table directly at Samantha. The girl’s eyes had become wider on hearing the room number.

“Oh, does he have a girlfriend staying with him? I’ve seen a blonde open the door to that room with a card key,” Becky said.

“Hmm. I don’t know about that, but whoever she is, that’s one lucky chick! See ya tomorrow!”

CHAPTER TWELVE

Becky and Samantha ambled along the seventeenth floor corridor without saying a word. They kept pace until they came near room 1792 where they slowed to a near-stop. Both of their heads turned at the same time to stare at the door to that mysterious room registered to Drew Lane. It was the room into which the well-dressed blonde woman had entered with her own key card. And it was potentially a room from which the professionally-styled green wig was found in the trash.

The quiet stroll was interrupted by an alert signal on Samantha's cell phone.

"Oh, I just got a text from my brother, Glen. He wants me to call him before I go to bed. I think he misses me."

"It's nice that you two are so close."

"Yeah, poor Glen is such a great person. He was born with a congenital spinal condition. He required special care and it was the breaking point for my parents. They already had their own bad habits that controlled their lives, in and out of rehab, in and out of jail. They finally got divorced when I was about eleven. My father's parents, my grandparents, knew we'd have a tough life, especially with Glen's special needs. My grandparents took custody of the two of us without any parental contesting. Then the rest is history."

The two stopped outside of Samantha's room in the corridor.

"Did you ever see your parents again after they split?" Becky asked.

"No. Grandpa had heard that my father was seriously ill in some hospital in southern California but we never learned where. The last I knew of my mother was that she was paroled from an Arizona state penitentiary, but her whereabouts were never known."

"Geez, I feel badly, Samantha. You really had a tough childhood. But I'm so happy to see you've taken such a crappy life and overcome all the challenges. You're a high school scholarship winner, you're going to a good college, and you still dedicate much of your life to your younger brother."

"Oh, he's self-sufficient in most things. And, he's become a great violinist. Next year he'll make first chair, second violin in the Evansville Symphony Orchestra. Does that makes any sense to you…being a flautist."

"It does! And that's impressive for such a young man."

As Samantha reached out to the room door with her card key, Becky grabbed her hand mid-air.

"What's wrong, Becky?"

"Hey, Samantha, I have an idea. Do you have Skype or some similar 'app' on your laptop in your room?"

"Ah, yeah, sure."

"Does Glen have it on his laptop back home?"

"Of course!"

"Tell him that he and I will do that duet tomorrow, but we can be with each other remotely via Skype. Tell him we'll perform ah…Debussy's Afternoon of a Fawn. I'm sure he knows it and has the music sheets for it."

“Wow, great idea! What time do you want to perform with Glen?”

“We’ll have some free time right after our breakfast talk. Tell him we’ll do it here in your room at…eleven.”

“And I’ll video record the piece to show others. Thanks, Becky!”

The two embraced briefly before Samantha opened her door.

Becky turned and headed for her own room, elated she could do something for her timid friend, Samantha, and her wheelchair-bound brother. She was excited that she was going to meet the talented young man and play a duet with him.

But her compassionate thoughts vanished when she opened the door to room 1775. A sealed envelope was on top of the sham at the head of the hotel bed.

Puzzled, she walked toward the bed and picked up the envelope with neat printing on the outside. “To Becky: from Mei Yang.”

Her mind quickly flashed to the hotel housekeeper she had greeted the other day.

She unsealed the envelope and pulled out a handwritten note. What surprised her was the text was not in English, but in traditional Chinese characters.

Becky,

My son, Daniel, works here at the hotel. He is a student at MIT but works nights in the hotel security office. I want him to introduce himself to you before you return home.

Thanks.

我的兒子，Daniel, 是上 MIT 的大學生. 他在警衛室上晚班的工作． 在你回家之前我想把他介紹給你.

謝謝！

Wǒ de érzi, Daniel, shì shàng MIT de dàxuéshēng. Tā zài jǐngwèi shì shàng wǎn bān de gōngzuò. Zài nǐ huí jiā zhīqián, wǒ xiǎng bǎ tā jièshào gěi nǐ.

Xiè xiè!

Becky smiled at the warm thoughtfulness of the older woman. She wondered if her son, Daniel, would be as sweet as this woman appeared to be. She put the note paper back into the envelope and placed it inside of her suitcase.

Then she sent out two text messages. One to her parents and one to Jake wishing them a good night and telling them she'd call them the next day.

* * *

The next morning brought another day of warm autumn sunshine to the Massachusetts capitol. Becky rose early and with running shorts and sleeveless shirt, she left the hotel to take a brief run around the city streets. With iPhone ear buds inserted, she rounded Copley Square then crossed over to Commonwealth Ave. The run was not only good for the cardiac exercise, but also provided another look at the city in which she hoped to become a college student within the next year.

She was amazed seeing the number of people already up and jogging in the city so soon after dawn. Most were in their twenties, many of them obviously college students. It was an adjustment to the inner city running, stopping at intersections then running in place until safe to cross the streets. The hub of Massachusetts was already busy early in the morning with vehicular traffic.

After nearly an hour, she returned to the hotel, pushing through the revolving glass door. As she smiled "good morning" at the registration desk staff dressed in uniforms, her eyes caught a sign on an adjacent door, "Security Office."

That must be where Mei Yang's son, Daniel, works. Maybe I'll say hello to him before I check out this week. His mom is so sweet.

The Abigail Adams meeting room was active with students coming in and heading immediately to the colorful breakfast buffet table. After getting a bowl of cold cereal and some fresh fruit, Becky found a couple of empty seats together. While she sat, she looked up and saw Brenda Cornwall carrying a small plate with a croissant and grapes.

The girl with the close-cropped haircut wore an expensive outfit of cardinal red-colored slacks, a linen top, and a matching scarf that encircled her neck then tied in a bow, covering her chest. The stylish outfit was obviously purchased from an upscale women's boutique.

Becky seized the opportunity.

"Oh, Brenda, this seat next to me is empty!"

Brenda looked down at Becky and smiled. She then pointed across to a single empty seat closer to the head table and next to Tran Nguyen. She smiled then mouthed the word, "thanks."

Hmm. I feel like I was just stood up. I wonder why she wants to sit closer to the podium. Or…is it the Vietnamese-American young man who has captured her interest?

Lynn Faulkner took the empty seat next to Becky.

"Hey, Lynn!"

"Hi, Becky! I wanted to ask you and Samantha a favor."

"What is it?"

Lynn's tone lowered to just above a whisper.

"It's about what I told you guys last night at the coffee shop. I don't want that story to get out. I thought it may have leaked out before I told you about the, ah…incident. But I spoke with Drew again this morning and he assured me that nobody knows about what I had done. He destroyed my phony ID and I feel good about that. But you two are the only ones who I told. So, I want to keep it that way if I can."

"Oh, sure. I'll tell Samantha to keep it quiet too. That's really cool of Drew to keep it quiet for you."

"You bet! I want to get a photo of me with him before the week ends. Hey, would you be willing to take a photo of the two us? I really want to shoot copies to my Facebook friends. Of course, I'll add my own personal caption."

"Sure! Just tell me when and where," Becky said with a grin.

"I have to ask him first. Of course, I'm sure that blonde you saw go into his room is his girlfriend, but hell, a girl like me can fantasize, right?"

Becky smiled at Lynn's candor. "That's right!"

After breakfast was done and plates cleared, Dr. Gleason stood up to get everyone's attention and to make her brief, daily announcements.

She then introduced a professor emeritus of American History from Harvard University who gave a funny and informative talk. It centered on the value of American History in secondary schools. He explained a new technique to teach history and how the traditional rote memorization of facts is less effective for students as the world becomes more technologically advanced.

While the talk was presented, Becky took a moment to pan around the tables at the student audience. The teenagers were riveted by the professor's every word. All of the teenagers, except for one.

Becky's eyes zoomed across the box-formation of tables at the well-dressed Brenda Cornwall. The girl was obviously disinterested in the talk and the eloquent speaker who stood only a few feet from her seat.

At one point the wealthy teen from New York looked around at the room of her peers. When she peered over at Becky, it appeared her eyes were glazed over with boredom. When the talk ended, Brenda was the first to leave the room before all others.

Becky joined Samantha to go back upstairs. Soon, they were on Skype with Samantha's brother.

"Okay, Glen. We can see you! Say hello to Becky."

After the introductions, Samantha prepared her video camera to record both Becky and her brother on the computer screen.

Moments later, the duo performed the classical piece; Glen on violin, Becky on flute. It was well done, and Samantha shouted out "Bravo, Bravo!" at the conclusion.

"Hey, Glen! Your sister just captured our duet performance on her camcorder. Now you can put it on Youtube and it'll go viral!"

"That's cool. I'm just happy and surprised she didn't drop the camera. She's likely to do that you know!" Glen said.

"Hey, you shush, Glen. And besides, Becky already knows I'm a klutz. She's seen me in action at the dinner table!"

They all laughed before logging off from the communications program. Becky carefully inserted her flute in its velvet-lined case.

"Hey, Beck, I've been trying to piece together why Green Hair used my identity when she met you in New Haven. Can we go over what took place last Saturday again, a little more slowly and with all the details?"

"Sure, why not?"

Samantha sat on her bed, while Becky sat in the room's leather chair and carefully reconstructed for her friend what had taken place that past Saturday morning.

She re-told everything, beginning with the flamboyant personality of the green-haired girl, and what had happened in the coffee shop.

Becky told her how the conversation had been tense with their probing questions to each other.

"But the whole scene imploded when she found out I was ethnic Chinese, Chinese-American."

"I just don't get that at all. Did you guys just get up and leave right then?"

Becky thought for a moment before answering.

"Ah, no. She stepped outside of the restaurant to make a phone call. She told me it was something personal and she had to call back home. She obviously needed some privacy for the call. All of a sudden that was very important to her; like an emergency."

"So when she brought her cell outside to make the call, could you see her?"

Becky's eyes opened wide.

"Hey, what's wrong, Beck?"

"You just made me remember something. It wasn't her cell phone. Green Hair's cell phone was dead. She asked to use my iPhone to make that call outside of the coffee shop. Do you know what that means?"

"Huh? No. What?"

"The phone number of whoever she called will still be on my phone. Let me check!"

Becky pulled out her iPhone from her small handbag and quickly began scrolling down a variety of screens.

"Hey, that's right. Just look for the area code of 812. That's the Evansville, Indiana number," Samantha suggested.

"Hmm, I can't find any calls with that area code. But there aren't too many calls listed here. Hey, wait! There's one here from last Saturday with a 617 code. I don't recognize that number."

"Yeah, 617. That's right here in Boston. You must've made a call to the hotel or some place around here before you drove up from Connecticut."

"No. I never made any calls to Boston. I had no reason to do that. I just drove directly up here on Sunday morning." Becky's eyes focused on her scrolling screen. "And here are all of my personal calls I made to my home after the '617' phone call. But this '617' number must have been the number that Green Hair called."

"Well, there's only one way to find out!" Samantha added.

"Yeah, but what do I say if she answers the phone? Or worse, what if it's her family home number? Maybe Green Hair isn't from Indiana, but lives right here in Boston."

"Let's call that phone number to find out. Put the cell on 'speaker' so we can both listen. If someone answers with a voice you don't recognize, just ask who it is and tell them you dialed the wrong number."

Becky put speaker on then anxiously called the number. The ringing sound echoed inside of the hotel room. After four loud rings, the call went to a voice mail answering greeting. The two girls listened together to the recorded greeting:

"Hello! You've reached Drew Lane. Leave a message, I'll get back."

CHAPTER THIRTEEN

After hearing the recorded greeting from a voice they both recognized, Becky immediately turned off her cell phone. Silence filled the room. For what seemed like a lifetime, she and Samantha just stared at one another from across the hotel room. It was evident each of them had a flurry of thoughts running through their young and nimble minds.

"Holy crap! What the hell does this all mean, Becky?"

"I…don't know. I mean, you heard it too. It seems Green Hair must have known Drew or at least was in contact with him before she and I sat down in that New Haven coffee shop Saturday morning."

"But she told you she had to make a very important call—back home to Indiana. She said it was critical, so much so, that she had to borrow your cell phone right away."

"That's right, she did," Becky replied.

"Then she stepped outside so you couldn't listen to the private conversation." Samantha shook her head back and forth, then stared back at her friend. "Well, now we know the bitch who stole my identity also lied to you. She sure as hell didn't call anyone at home in Indiana."

"You're right. But let's use some logic here. Yes, she lied to me and she didn't call home, wherever her home really is. But what bothers me is this whole thing started right after she discovered that I am Asian, when I took off my sunglasses and she saw that I'm Chinese. Why did that one thing trigger her to morph into a whole different and weird personality? She suddenly became…I don't know, angry, like she was pissed that I wasn't a Caucasian. Then, all of a sudden, she dropped the theatrical personality and became, you know, more serious, and….more concerned about making that phone call right away."

"And believe me; I understand how that whole racist scene bothers you. But do you know what bothers me?" Samantha asked.

"What?"

Samantha's eyes gave away her anxiety before she spoke. "That green wig we found in the trash bag. It may have come from room 1792, Drew Lane's room."

"Hmm. I thought about that. It does seem coincidental, doesn't it?"

"Coincidental? I think it's freakin' creepy!"

"But how would he get a hold of the green wig? Unless…she's with him. But why would she be here at the hotel with Drew?"

"I think that's what we have to find out."

The Abigail Adams room was filled with a more casual atmosphere later that day. This conference session was intended to be less formal, according to the Scholarship Program pamphlet.

All of the students and faculty dressed down, wearing blue jeans, shorts, and casual shirts. The buffet luncheon featured New England clam chowder, native lobster salad, cranberry-apple salad, tuna salad, local cod cakes, Boston baked beans, and other varieties of mid-day fare common from the state of Massachusetts.

Becky and Samantha filled their trays and carried them to the square formation of tables. Already seated was the quiet Brenda Cornwall. Becky sat on one side of the wealthy New Yorker, Samantha on the other side.

"Hi, Brenda, I'm Samantha. Are you still unable to speak?"

Brenda nodded her head in the affirmative with a smile exposing her braces.

The socialite had changed into a green jersey and tight-fitting stylish blue jeans. But now she had a new silk scarf of green, white, and blue that complimented her jersey. Just as earlier, the scarf was wrapped around her neck and tied in a knot at her chest. A green eye shadow complimented her top, but her tinted glasses minimized the effect.

"Oh, that's too bad."

Brenda then jotted down a question on her pad of paper.

What are the titles of your scholarship papers?

Samantha answered quickly. "Oh, my paper is on the President Ronald Reagan administration. My title is 'The Great Communicator—New Leader or an Old Actor?' It's a series of personal anecdotes about the President, later called 'The Great Communicator.'"

Brenda gave a thumbs up along with a braces-filled smile at the catchy title.

"And mine is about Paul Revere and his midnight ride to start the Revolutionary War. My submitted paper is titled 'Paul Revere's Ride—Poetry or History?" said Becky. "Hey, how about you, Brenda? What's your paper about?"

Brenda scribbled on the notepad then showed it to the two girls on either side of her. Her handwritten note read:

The Original Thirteen—not so cozy colonies.

"Hey, that sounds like that could be interesting! I bet you did a lot of research on that, huh?" Becky said.

Brenda nodded her head, fluttering her eyelids laden with green eye shadow.

Before the luncheon came to a close, wait staff came around offering hot tea or coffee. Both Becky and Samantha asked for tea, while Brenda declined.

Dr. Brooke Gleason stood up, dressed in a black polo shirt and casual white linen slacks. Her outfit once again complimented the attractive woman's curvy, fit body.

"So we're now officially half-way through our Scholarship Program and it's been a pleasure getting to know each of you. You are all bright and deserving students and I know you will all do well in your college pursuits. And I am glad that each of you could attend the program here in Boston that we organize each year. I do hope you tell your teachers and administrators about your experience to cultivate more interest for the underclassmen to compete in the years ahead."

Just as Dr. Gleason was about to conclude her inspirational speech, Samantha picked up her cup to take a sip of the hot tea.

But when she tried to pick up the porcelain cup, it slipped from her crooked finger and spilled. The hot liquid flooded toward Brenda who was staring straight ahead. The steaming tea ran off the table and onto Brenda's lap.

"Owww! Goddamnit! That's hot!" Brenda screamed. Her loud outburst startled the attendees.

Samantha nervously stood up to help her victim.

"Oh my God. I am so sorry. It…it was an accident. I'm so damn clumsy! I'm sorry. Here, let me get more cloth napkins."

A waitress ran over to the table and quickly cleaned up the spill while Brenda stood up. She blotted the dark wet stain on the front of her faded blue jeans with her cloth napkin. There was no attempt to hide the annoyed expression on her face.

"I'm sorry, Brenda," Samantha said once again.

Brenda simply picked up her handbag. She violently threw the damp, tea-stained napkin onto the table then hurried out of the Abigail Adams room.

Becky panned around at the students and faculty seated at the box diagram of tables. The quiet hung in the ballroom air for several moments until Samantha sat down once again.

"Ah, is everything all right over there?" Dr. Gleason asked from across the room.

"Yes, yes. It was just a small accident," Samantha responded.

Dr. Gleason resumed her talk. She reminded everyone to have their five minute talk prepared for the Thursday evening dinner program. She explained that there would be about fifty additional invited guests in the audience—mostly history professors from the nearby colleges and universities; they were excited to listen to each student present a brief synopsis of their research papers that had won them the prized scholarship.

"And there will also be other docents in the audience from some of the historical museums and landmark sites from New England. It should be exciting," Brooke added. "And please dress accordingly. It will be a sit-down dinner and after dessert is served, we will begin the program. I will introduce each student with the title of your paper and then you will approach the podium. If there are any questions, please contact me or Drew Lane.

On the following Friday morning, we'll have an informal breakfast and closing remarks. We also have a gift basket of sorts for each of you. It's a modest package of mementoes and gifts from the event and your stay here in old Bean Town!

Now the afternoon for today is free time. You all know about the tours that are available, including the famous 'Duck Tours' that are both interesting and fun!

I know some of you are anxious to visit some of the nearby college campuses. When you arrive at the campus there might be tours available, but you can certainly explore on your own.

"So, people, we won't meet again until tomorrow morning for our next breakfast meeting. For now, enjoy your afternoon and evening in Boston or Cambridge and we'll see you all tomorrow!"

Samantha stayed close to Becky as the crowd left the conference room. The two walked together into the lobby without saying a word and headed directly toward the elevator.

"I just feel like such an ass! I guess I really pissed off Brenda when I spilled my tea onto her. She didn't look happy when she left in a huff."

"Oh, don't worry about it. Just let it go, Samantha. You apologized to her. It was a freaking accident, for God's sake. I just think that New York chick is uptight about something. She never pays attention to what's being said or going on with the program. It's almost as if she never wanted to be here."

"Man! She surprised me with her reaction though. I thought we were all friends here. She's the only one who turns me off. Wow, did she yell out when that hot tea spilled onto her lap!"

Becky looked over at her friend. "Yeah. I'm amazed she could shout out so loudly for a girl who has laryngitis. Her voice was crystal clear and loud, when I heard her."

Samantha returned Becky's stare without saying a word.

"Hey, guys, over here!" came a voice from behind them. It was Lynn catching up with them. Her tight-fitting pink jersey topped a pair of tan short shorts.

"Hey, I spoke with Drew. He told me I could have a picture taken with him this afternoon. So can I ask one of you to take a picture with my camera?"

"Sure, Lynn! Just tell us when and where," said Becky.

"Oh, that's easy. The when is now, and the where is upstairs in his hotel room. Let's go!"

Samantha's eyes met Becky's as the three of them quietly took the elevator up to room 1792.

The three girls stood in the hotel corridor while Lynn tapped on the door.

When the door opened, Drew seemed surprised that Lynn was joined by others. He had on a plaid shirt and blue-jeans.

"Oh! Hi, girls! Are you all here for photographs?"

"Ah, yeah, sure," Samantha replied.

"I already had one earlier of Drew and me on the tour, but now your goatee is darker and thicker, so it'll look like I'm with a different guy," Becky said boldly.

The group giggled at the remark.

"Okay. So where would you like the pictures taken? I can put on a sweater and we can go outside the hotel, if you'd like."

Lynn instantly shot her opened palm in the air.

"Ah, no, no! I think we can do it right here in your room, Drew. It's just a picture to bring back with us so when we mention your name, people can put a face to you."

Drew turned to straighten up some newspapers on top of the bureau while responding.

"Oh, sure. But don't forget Brooke Gleason and Helen Brisbane. I'm sure they'd be happy to have their mugs in a photo with you."

Lynn gave Becky and Samantha a quick wink.

"Great idea, Drew! We'll be sure to do that," Lynn said with a grin.

They used the wide window of the hotel room as a backdrop for the photo. At seventeen stories high, it offered a spectacular view of the city of Boston and beyond.

First, Samantha posed, standing next to Drew very close, one hand behind his back. Then Becky took her turn, showing her dimples with a happy smile.

But when it was time for Becky to snap the photo of Drew and Lynn together, the young girl snuggled closer to the handsome man with the red-brown goatee.

"All done," Becky said. "That should come out nice!"

"Oh, one more, just one more, Becky," Lynn begged.

Once again, Becky focused the camera at the attractive couple posing in the room.

"Okay, smile," Becky said.

Just before Becky pressed the button, Lynn quickly turned to Drew and kissed him near his lips.

Click.

"Hey! What's that all about?" he asked.

"That was just a little 'thank you kiss' for helping me out when I needed you."

"Oh," Drew responded with a cautious smile.

Lynn giggled once again as she grabbed her camera back from Becky. Within minutes, the trio had thanked Drew and left room 1792.

When they stepped into the hallway, they nearly bumped into Mei Yang who was pushing her housekeeping cart. When she saw the three girls, she nodded and smiled.

"Hello, Becky," the older woman said in English.

"你好" Nǐ hǎo, (Hello)," Becky replied.

"Come, Becky, let's check out the pics inside my room," Lynn said as she opened her hotel room door. The other two followed.

Mei Yang took her cell phone from her uniform pocket and made a call.

Moments later the girls were trading cameras to look at the digital photos.

"This is great! Now I have lots of stories to tell my friends back in Santa Fe with this pic of me and Drew!" exclaimed Lynn.

"Just don't let them put it on Facebook!" Samantha cautioned.

"Why not? It's all in fun!"

Later, Becky ambled back to her own hotel room. Just before sliding her card key into the door slot, she heard her name called out.

"Becky? Are you Becky Bing?"

She slowly turned to become face to face with someone she didn't know.

"Oh, hi! Yes, I'm Becky. Becky Bing."

She extended her hand to the handsome young man who quickly reached out to shake it.

"I'm Daniel Yang. You know my mother who works up here. And I work here at the hotel on most nights. But I'm a college student by day."

The two chatted in the hallway for several minutes. The handsome Chinese-American, a sophomore at MIT, told her of his work in the hotel security office.

"I really like working here. Not only do I back up the computer systems on the night shift, but I'm also responsible for the security surveillance image data. All of the security cameras take digital recordings. Then I download them to disks and catalogue them and all that stuff."

Becky explained to the young man with a warm smile how that afternoon was free time for the student scholars and she had planned on visiting the Harvard campus, not far from Harvard on the Cambridge side of the Charles River.

"Hey, I know the Harvard campus very well! I spend a lot of time there with my buds. Why don't you let me show you around?"

The invitation was sincerely cordial and his inviting eyes told her she should take advantage of this kind offer.

Becky did an about face, not turning into her room, but walking down the corridor with Daniel Yang at her side. As they turned the corner, she saw something that made her come to an abrupt stop.

The door to room 1790 opened and out stepped the mysterious blonde, still with large sunglasses, now dressed in white slacks topped with a navy-blue shirt blouse. The blue was matched with the color of her trendy Converse sneakers. She carried a red leather bag.

As the blonde checked her hotel room door to ensure it was locked, she turned to face Becky and Daniel standing in the hallway. She quickly turned away and headed briskly toward the bank of elevators.

"Is there something wrong, Becky?" Daniel asked.

Becky realized she was still in the halted position. She then resumed walking slowly, staring at the room number to double check it was not 1792.

"Oh, ah, no. It's just that I've seen that blonde before, but previously she had opened the door to room 1792, Drew Lane's room. But today she's coming out of room 1790." She turned to face Daniel. "Oh, I'm sorry. Drew Lane is one of the faculty assigned to our conference this week."

"And she's not part of the conference program?"

"No. I never saw her before at any sessions. But I think she's been here all week."

"Maybe she and this Drew are friends. Those two rooms are adjoining, you know. They have a door that connects both of them."

"Aha, as a hotel security guy, you'd know that, eh?" Becky winked.

"Yeah. I have to know pretty much everything that has to do with the safety of the hotel guests. My boss has been a wicked, awesome mentor and a real nice guy. It's not Computer Science, which is my passion, but I still enjoy my night-time job here."

The two stepped through the large, glass revolving door and onto the historical Copley Square. Daniel escorted her on the brief walk to the MBTA subway station. They took the "Red Line" commuter train to Harvard Square where they began the tour surrounded by students, professors, and administrators enjoying the warm fall afternoon.

Becky enjoyed strolling through the famous Harvard Yard with its old, overgrown shade trees that outlined the perimeter of the square. Many tour groups, led by entertaining undergraduate students' guides, learned of the rich history of the campus; including its humorous tales and legends.

Becky was thoroughly enjoying the information and the fun walk with the handsome and outgoing Daniel Yang. She found him to be funny, polite, and sensitive to those things she was interested in seeing. He was an excellent escort bringing her into buildings and places not normally accessible to tourists.

They bumped into a couple of his friends along their tour. One was another budding scientist, Kelly Ling, an attractive girl from Beijing. They spoke in Mandarin when they chatted in the campus courtyard. Kelly was nice but seemed to veil an inner jealousy upon seeing the adorable Becky with her close friend.

The other friend was a student from the Ukraine. Ivan and Daniel shared a keen interest in sports.

The two took a break and had iced tea at one of the cafes in Harvard Square. Based on the crowd, it was one of the more popular spots with the local students. Later, they went down into the subway tunnel, jumped on a car, and headed back to the hotel.

Standing in the hotel lobby, Becky held out her hand for Daniel to shake and thanked him for his kindness.

He took her hand in his and held it for a long time.

"It was my pleasure, Becky. I enjoyed the time and being with you. Thank you! Let me ask, what are you doing with your free time tonight? Are you going to some of the museums, or maybe the symphony? Symphony Hall is just down the street. I know you're just eighteen, so hitting the clubs is probably not your thing."

"Ah, I haven't thought about tonight, yet, but I'll get out of here to get a bite to eat. Is there a good Chinese restaurant around here?"

Daniel answered with a grin. "Well, the best Chinese food I know of can be found inside my mom's kitchen. But Chinatown isn't too far from here."

The two split up to go their separate ways. Daniel stepped into the Security Office to begin his work while Becky headed up to the seventeenth floor.

CHAPTER FOURTEEN

When she arrived inside room 1775, her first thought was to flop on the bed and think about what she was doing. With a whirlwind of emotions including guilt, she pulled out her cell and called Jake.

"Hey, Babe! What's up?"

"Where are you, Jake?"

"I'm at work. They asked me to work 'til nine tonight. I just ended my break and right now I'm heading out to the floor. I have a bunch of kids' footballs and helmets to set up in the display shelves before I leave tonight."

"Oh, I won't keep you. But can we talk later?"

"Sure. But, hey, wait. Tell me about your new boyfriend!"

Becky's heart stopped. Her face flushed with a fleeting sense of guilt.

What? What the hell is he talking about? I just went for a couple of hours with Daniel to see the college campus. How in God's name could he ever know I was just with him?

"Huh? What are you talking about?"

"You know what I mean. It's that cute guy who you and all the girls are swooning over. What's his name? Drew? Is it Drew Lane?"

"Oh, God! Drew? Hey, I don't swoon over him. But I tell you what. I have some photos of him with us girls and an earlier one I took at the Old North Church. I'll send them to you and you can see he's way too old and clearly not my type."

"Oh? And what is your type?" Jake asked with a chuckle.

"I'll tell you later. Hey, your break is over. Get back to work!"

"Just one thing, Becky. You know I'm only kidding about this Drew character. I really want you to enjoy your week up there and please just see everything you can while you have the chance. Don't miss out on anything!"

Just as she hung up, there was another call on her cell. It was from a Boston number.

"Hello."

"Hello. This is Drew."

"Oh, hello, Drew. What's up?"

"What's up? Yeah, what is up? Who is this?"

Becky's eyebrows furled into a confused expression. "Huh? Drew, it's me, Becky. Becky Bing." She chuckled. "You called me. What's this about?"

"Oh, ah, Becky. You must have called me earlier on this cell; my, ah, private cell phone. There was no message, so I just called that number to see who was trying to contact me."

Becky's mind flashed, looking for some creative way to respond. "Oh, my bad. That was a mistake. I didn't mean to call you. Sorry, I should have left a message."

"Hmm. See, Becky, I'm a little confused. This is a very private number. I've only had it for about two weeks. Only a few people know it. So, how did you get this number?"

Becky suddenly felt her mouth getting dry as she heard his voice become stern and irritated. It suddenly became difficult to swallow.

"Oh, ah, believe me, Drew, it's kind of a long story and right now I'm on my way out."

Pause.

"Well, I'd like to hear that long story when we meet again, Becky. It's important that I know who has this private number."

"Sure, sure, Drew. We'll do that!"

After disconnecting, Becky fell backwards on her bed.

Holy shit! What am I going to tell him? Should I say I made a mistake and dialed the wrong number? Hell no, that's just too convenient and he'd never believe it. Do I tell him about Green Hair who used my phone to call him from New Haven? But if he has given his new cell number to only a handful of people, and Green Hair was one of the chosen few, those two obviously know each other.

Becky massaged her forehead with her fingertips to ease the tension headache building, combined with hunger pains.

The loud ringing of the hotel room phone startled her once again.

She looked at the red light blinking each time it rang. Finally, she reached out and picked up the handset.

"Hey, Beck! It's Daniel. I'm downstairs and my boss gave me the night off. How would you like me to take you to Chinatown now for a good meal? It's my treat!"

"Oh, Daniel, I…I really…"

He cut her off mid-sentence. "And then there's one historical landmark site in Boston you absolutely have to see before you drive back home to Connecticut. And I'd love to bring you there!"

"Oh, really? Where is this historical landmark I should see?"

"It's not far away. It's Fenway Park, the oldest major league baseball stadium in America and the home of the Boston Red Sox for one hundred years."

Becky started giggling, hearing his proud and boastful answer.

"But Daniel, how do we get into Fenway Park at night?"

"Simple. There's a game there tonight with the Los Angeles Angels. And do you remember my friend, Ivan, who we met briefly today over at Harvard?"

"Yes, of course, the student from the Ukraine."

"It turns out Ivan had two tickets for tonight's game but he can't go, so he gave them to me. C'mon, we'll have some good Asian food and then take the 'T' to Kenmore Square. Fenway Park is just a block from there. It's part of your educational tour of Boston before you have to leave."

The cheery voice and invitation diverted her attention from Drew's disturbing phone call. And then she remembered what Jake had told her before they hung up. His voice rang clear in her mind as she recalled his message.

I hope you enjoy your week up there and please see everything you can while you have the chance. Don't miss out on anything!

"Hey, you know what, Daniel? I think I'll take you up on your invitation. Just give me about a half-hour and I'll meet you down in the lobby."

She was still troubled by Drew's phone call as she washed up and changed into khaki slacks and a bright red polo shirt. She left her room. Walking along the corridor, she restrained herself from glancing again at room 1792 when she passed by.

Becky loved seeing Boston's Chinatown. She was amazed at the colors of signs, restaurants, and silk banners blowing in the wind. They walked along Tyler St. enjoying the culinary scents and brightly decorated sights inside the Boston enclave with a variety of restaurants. There was Chinese, Mongolian, Japanese, and Malaysian cuisine to tempt any epicure. At an intersection, they turned onto Beach Street. This street had a more eclectic feel to it with its tiny shops, electronics stores, eateries, salons, grocery stores, and more.

"There's a lot of history to this Chinatown, Becky. Some very good, some not so good. But the fact that it's still here with all its pride and past is something that always impresses me."

Daniel then led her to a spot he was familiar with and which was highly recommended by the locals. The New Golden Gate restaurant had an extensive menu with reasonable prices and friendly service.

After a mix of dumplings, fried rice, and vegetables, 餃子炒米飯和蔬菜, Jiǎozi chǎo mǐfàn hé shūcài, served at their linen-covered table, the two young patrons dove into their plates full of delicious food. But never did the two stop talking.

After their meal, they opened their fortune cookies to find the entertaining messages inside.

"You go first," Becky told Daniel.

He unraveled the thin strip of paper.

"Okay. Mine says: 'You are on the correct path right now that will lead to mutual happiness.'" Daniel looked across the table with wide grin. "Now that sounds promising!"

They both smiled at each other for a moment without speaking.

Becky unraveled her fortune message.

"Mine says: 'You will have a mysterious and dangerous journey before you are finally satisfied,'" Becky read aloud.

"Now that sounds intriguing," he commented.

"Yeah, but not nearly as intriguing as your message!"

It was his turn to look into her eyes to interpret the message.

"Oh, I wanted to tell you about something I did while I was in the Security Office today."

"Really? What was it?" Becky asked.

"Well, I knew you were puzzled about that blonde woman you had seen coming and going into both rooms 1792 and 1790. So, since I have access to all of the guest data in the hotel, I did a search to see who had registered into those rooms."

Becky gently placed her chopsticks down on the side of her plate. She reached for a cup of the warm tea and looked across at the young man with the seductive smile, anxious to hear what he'd learned.

"I found out that room 1792 is registered to your faculty member, Mr. Drew Lane."

"Yes. I learned that a while ago. But what about room number 1790?"

"That room is registered to a female also assigned to your Scholars Program. Her name is Brenda Cornwall from Westchester County up in New York. Both rooms became occupied on the same date. It was last Sunday around noontime."

"Brenda Cornwall? Daniel, with due respect to the hotel's database, there's something wrong there. Brenda Cornwall had a serious throat infection and couldn't join the conference until Tuesday night. She didn't arrive until sometime on Tuesday. And Brenda has very short hair, almost a buzz-cut. The woman I was confused about was a thick-haired blonde, perhaps a few years older than those of us invited to the conference."

"Hmm," replied Daniel, obviously disappointed.

"But it's hard to tell what she looked like. She always wore nice outfits with big, dark sunglasses. And she moves quickly. Like I told you, I saw her coming out of room 1790 and also saw her opening the door to room 1792. So this blonde apparently has cardkeys for both."

"Well, that's the name in the system."

"Do you think this mystery blonde might be Drew's girlfriend who just wanted to have her own private room…for some strange reason?"

Becky blushed after asking the question.

"I never try to figure those things out. Maybe Drew snores loudly or has insomnia and is awake all night or something like that. Perhaps separate rooms would make their stay more…I don't know, pleasurable?"

"Yeah, sure, the snoring at night. That must be it," Becky responded.

They both stared at each other in silence. Then they burst out laughing.

"Do you know anything about this Brenda?" Daniel asked.

"Only that she comes from one of the wealthiest families in America."

"Maybe my mom knows something since she cleans that block of rooms. I might ask her what she may have seen, if anything."

The Red Sox beat the Angels 4-3 in the ninth inning. Becky loved the energy and the enthusiasm of the Boston fans. The herds of people, many dressed in bright red shirts, came out of the landmark baseball park in a celebratory mood. The yelling and screaming echoed along the city streets in the warm, fall evening. The streets seemed liked a moving river of crimson.

Becky was impressed at how Daniel had been a gentleman during the entire evening. The new friend and excitement temporarily took her thoughts off of Green Hair, Drew's phone call, and the mysterious blonde. They continuously laughed and joked, sometimes in Mandarin, but most of the time in English.

Later in the evening, when he escorted her to the door to her room, Daniel appeared nervous about how to say goodnight. It was the first time each of them had struggled to find words with one another.

He put his hand out to shake, but something stirred in Becky. She did something uncharacteristic for her persona. Instead of grasping his hand, she reached up to his smooth, bronze face. Gently taking his face inside both of her soft hands, she gently lowered his head down to hers. They both closed their eyes and shared a soft but sincere kiss.

Becky smiled a "goodnight." As she turned away, she swiped her card key. Once inside room 1775, she locked the door and fell once again, spread-eagled into her bed. Her mind spun with all that was happening to her during her week in Boston.

She looked at the digital clock on the nightstand. It was just eleven. After a deep breath, she called Jake.

"Hey, I went to Fenway Park tonight. It was great!"

"Good for you! I liked that stadium when I was up that way. Hey, I got your pictures. It looks like you're taking in a lot of sights. And I see why the girls like Drew. He's a good-looking guy but for some weird reason he looks familiar to me."

"Familiar? How? He's from around here."

"I noticed he's been growing a goatee. But it's the first photo taken near the Old North Church, with the growth just starting, where he looks familiar."

"Hmm. That's funny. Yeah, that was Monday, first full day here and the day we took his Boston tour."

"But there seems to be a dark spot in the middle of his new goatee. What's that about?"

"Oh, yeah. He has a deep, cleft chin. You know, like what some kids call a 'butt chin.'"

"Cleft chin, a cleft chin. Now I remember! Becky, listen to me. Do you remember last Saturday at the New Haven train station? I was ready to take a picture of you standing next to Green Hair. But as I got the right focus, some guy came by and accidentally knocked the camera out of my hands."

"Yeah, yeah. I remember how you got bumped. The camera went flying so you couldn't take the picture. By the time you got recomposed, our Indiana girl had slipped away."

"Well, the guy who hit me had a very noticeable cleft chin. And his expression, especially around the mouth in your pictures, looks just like that same guy. Do you think that Drew was with Green Hair that Saturday?"

Becky's mind started whirring. "Together? Both in New Haven at the same time? I…I don't know. What else do you remember about this guy?"

"Not much. I was so pissed he bumped into me. He had on dark sunglasses. Let's see. He also wore a brown leather jacket, blue jeans and oh, yeah, a baseball cap."

"Hmm. Was it a Red Sox cap?"

"No. It was navy blue with the light blue letters 'C U' on it. It wasn't a professional team. I'm pretty sure it was a college ball cap. Hold on while I Google to see if I can find a cap image like that."

Becky put the phone on speaker as she began to strip down for bed. Soon, she heard Jake's voice once again.

"Hey, I got it! I just matched the same cap that guy wore. It's a college hat all right, but this university isn't up there in Boston. In fact, it's not even in Massachusetts. It's in New York."

Becky's heart pounded with anticipation, and then she asked her question.

"Oh, no. Is it Columbia University?"

"It sure as hell is! His hat was the official baseball cap for Columbia."

"Oh my God! Drew Lane was working on his doctoral degree—at Columbia."

CHAPTER FIFTEEN

Becky had difficulty falling asleep that night. She thought about Drew Lane possibly linked with Green Hair during the New Haven visit. The phone call the imposter made using Becky's phone confirmed she had known Drew; a complex character playing as a faculty member, Boston tour guide, and conference security guy.

If that was Drew, and he wasn't up here in Boston at the time of the phone call, he and Green Hair were both in New Haven together.

Becky may have learned more about the bizarre puzzle but this one only led her to more questions. While she lay in the bed she tried to sort things out.

What the hell did this wacko, Green Hair, and PhD candidate, Drew Lane, have in common? What could this odd couple be up to in this weird imposter scheme?

And why did Green Hair tell me she was Samantha Rawlings from Indiana? What was she really looking for me? And why did she back off and get upset after seeing I'm a Chinese-American?

Why the hell did she go out of her way to meet me before coming up here to the conference?

And what's the connection with this freakin' weird blonde here on the seventeenth floor and the mysterious Brenda Cornwall?

She kicked off her bed covers, got up from bed, and stepped over to the room's desk, switching on the lamp. After pulling out her notebook, she jotted down those same questions that niggled at her brain.

It wasn't until 2AM when she finally fell asleep.

* * *

It was cloudy when Becky arose the next morning and stepped outside for her early run. She followed the same jogging loop as the other morning and headed for the home stretch to the hotel when a steady drizzle began to dampen her clothes and her spirits.

When she had jogged to just a few blocks away from the hotel, a familiar voice called out her name. It came from a short distance behind her.

"Hey, Becky! Hold up!"

She stopped and turned. It was Drew Lane, dressed in running gear and apparently finishing his early morning jog.

"Oh, good morning, Drew!"

He quickly caught up to her. The two walked quickly side by side up to the hotel.

"I just wanted to follow up on our conversation. When I found that it was you who called my private line, it just blew my mind. And I know it wasn't me who gave the number to you."

"Yeah, you told me that your private number was known by only a few close friends."

"So, tell me. Where did you get my cell number?"

They each took turns entering the hotel, stepping through the massive, revolving glass door.

Once indoors, the two walked side by side a short distance until they stopped in front of the small newsstand located midway into the hotel lobby.

"Like I told you, it's kind of a long, involved story."

"Becky, I just want a name. Of the three people who I gave it to, I just want to know which one gave it to you. And, of course, I'd like to learn why that individual gave it to you."

Becky was becoming angry at the probing interrogation.

"Drew, the truth is I don't know who gave it to me."

She noticed how quickly the color of his face deepened into an inflamed red.

"What? C'mon, Becky. That's total bullshit and you know it! You must've had some contact with the person who gave you the number."

"Your number wasn't given to me. Look. Someone asked to borrow my cell phone to make, what she told me, was an important call. Apparently, the number she called turned out to be yours. After she returned my cell, I paid no attention to who the hell she called but it was stored on my phone."

"But you called me the other night. What was that about?"

Becky took a deep breath before she spoke to the man with the intense expression on his face.

"Listen. I was about to make a call while I was talking to someone. I was trying to call the store where I work part-time, back home. Not paying enough attention, I scrolled down through some stored numbers to make a call and I apparently selected your number left on my cell by mistake," she lied.

"Becky, what was the person's name who asked to borrow the phone?"

The conversation had just reached the point of no return. But she had to be cautious. She didn't want to disclose that she was now aware Drew had apparently been in the New Haven train station with Green Hair. She had to think quickly before answering.

Shit! I'm in a tight corner right now with no options. I've got to tell him. There's no sense keeping this weird thing my secret any longer. I'll just tell him what happened.

"Look, Drew, some kook, some…I don't know…weird girl met me in Connecticut last weekend. She told me she was Samantha Rawlings from Indiana and on her way to this conference. We met and had a cup of coffee in a restaurant. After we chatted, she told me she had to make an important call back home because her cell was dead. She asked to use my phone and I gave it to her. She stepped outside of the coffee shop and evidently tapped in the new '617' number; your private number.

"She came back in, returned my phone to me, and told me she had to leave right away. I figured there were some personal problems back home and escorted her back to the station. She ran to catch her train. I thought I'd meet her up here again, but as it turns out, she never came here. The girl with green hair was an imposter. I met the real Samantha Rawlings the first night I was here and believe her to be the real girl from Evansville, Indiana."

While she spoke, Becky kept relentless eye contact with Drew. She noticed his expression change from one of anger into one of complete surprise.

"Hmm. Well, that is strange, because I never spoke with anyone on this phone last Saturday. If you don't know who this…this imposter was then we don't know how she got the phone number, do we? Maybe she called then knew she misdialed and hung up. So, I'll just let it go."

Becky stared with a suspicious eye at the man who had just lied to her to bail his ass out of a compromising position.

You lying son of a bitch! I know you were in New Haven with this chick, whoever she is. I saw her make that one call. I don't know what's going on here yet, mister, but I'm sure as hell going to find out!

"Yeah, I guess we'll just let it go, Drew."

Drew's eyes were now riveted onto her eyes. For a moment they stared at each other without a word. But the silence spoke volumes of what was happening with this twisted mystery with the American History Scholarship Program.

The moment became tense as they both strutted to the elevator.

Just before the door closed, one more passenger slipped in.

"Daniel!"

The young man turned to see Becky in her dampened running outfit.

"Hey, Becky! Looks like you got wet during your run! It's really pouring out now!"

Becky's eyes caught Daniel's eyes then swiveled them toward Drew.

The young Chinese-American man picked up on the silent signal. He recognized the man with the goatee and turned to face the elevator doors without any more dialogue.

The elevator car made several stops with people getting on or off at various floors. At the seventeenth floor, Drew got off quickly and headed for his room at a brisk pace. Daniel and Becky ambled slowly along the carpeted corridor.

"I'm guessing that guy you looked at is Drew Lane, is it not?" Daniel asked in a low whisper.

"Yeah. We just had a really intense conversation."

"Did he upset you?"

"Ah, yes and no. It's a long and bizarre mystery that I'm trying to solve."

"Hey, I enjoy long and bizarre mysteries. Does it have something to do with those two adjacent rooms on this floor and that blonde woman who bothers you so much?"

Becky stopped in her footsteps. She stared into space, struck by a thought.

"Hmm. Yes, yes, it does in a way, but this mystery didn't start here on the seventeenth floor. It started last week, back in my hometown in Connecticut."

"Even more intriguing, crossing interstate lines. That's cool."

Becky smiled at her new friend.

Daniel pulled out a pen and a small notepad and jotted something .

"What are you writing?"

"Here's my cell number," he told her. "Text me or call me. I have today off since it's a so-called 'reading day' for us to study. We have to prep for mid-terms coming up next week. I just have to find my mom and give her something she left at home earlier this morning. Maybe you and I could do something if you get some free time."

"Hey, I'd like that! We just have a breakfast meeting and then we have to give our five-minute presentations later tonight. I'll be free about ten. Do you want to do something?"

Daniel turned to her with a grin on his face.

"Yes. But I just want to do one particular thing."

"Huh? What's that?"

"I want for you and me to go someplace where you can tell me this long and bizarre mystery you're struggling with. I want to see if maybe I can help you solve it."

Becky turned to him with a warm smile then headed toward Room 1775.

* * *

After showering, Becky called her parents again at home. They put on their speaker phone so they could both talk with her. They were anxious to see her return home but knew in her voice she was enjoying the special event in Boston.

"And, Mom, I met a nice guy up here!"

Silence. "Oh?"

"His name is Daniel. He's a sophomore at MIT. He works at this hotel. I met him through his mother."

There was another quiet pause on both ends of the line for an extended moment.

"Oh, well, that's nice, Sweetie. You know your dad and I always trust your judgment in friends. Just please be careful up there."

Becky didn't want to expand on the topic. She changed subjects, asking about things at home. She then reminded them about the evening's event with a large audience to hear the scholars' presentations.

"I'm sure you'll do well, Becky. I wish we could be there to support you and listen, but it's not possible."

"Oh, that's okay. There won't be many friends or family members in the audience."

"Ah, what about Jake?" Mrs. Bing asked. "Can he make it up there for the special event?"

A smile graced Becky's face after her mom's leading question, no doubt curious about the current status of her six-month relationship with Jake.

"Ah, no. Actually, he and his mom are leaving for a flight back to Colorado and won't be back until Monday."

"Oh. Well, good luck tonight, Sweetie, and please call to let us know how it went!"

The Abigail Adams Room had a different look to it on this Thursday morning. The breakfast buffet table had been re-located in a far corner of the carpeted and elegant ballroom. Stacks of chairs were lined up against the wall. The preparations for the evening event were cued with anticipation of an audience of nearly one hundred people.

Becky chose to sit next to Tran Nguyen. She was interested in his background and his parents coming to America from South Vietnam.

"I really had a great childhood, Becky. My family was always supportive of me in school, despite their struggles with the English language. They also encouraged my interest in music which I hope to continue after high school."

Dr. Gleason stood up at the head table and asked for everyone's attention.

"I'll be brief since today is our last formal day of the program with our dinner event tonight. We all look forward to hearing your individual presentations tonight. Tomorrow is simply a casual breakfast meeting. I know some of you will not be here because of buses, planes, or trains to catch to head back home. But it is a chance to say goodbye to the new friends we've all made here this week."

As Becky listened, she looked around at the seated students. There was one chair empty between Lynn and James. One student hadn't shown up yet. She quickly looked around at all of the faces to account for the students. The missing student was once again Brenda Cornwall.

Dr. Gleason continued.

"Now I have one announcement that is quite exciting! The hotel has made our organization a generous offer. If any of you students want to stay in Boston for the remainder of the weekend, the hotel will allow you to keep your same room until Sunday afternoon, meaning you can stay here, free of charge for Friday and Saturday night!

"If you're going to stay beyond tomorrow, you must contact the front desk and let them know when you expect to leave. Of course, Dr. Brisbane, Drew, and I will no longer be here. So you'll be on your own and I expect you will contact your families to let them know of your arrangements. Now, are there any questions about this evening's dinner and presentations?"

James raised his hand. "Is there a specific order that we follow to get up to the podium to give our talk?"

"Well, I can leave that up to all of you. You'll have a choice. We can go in alphabetical order, or pick numbers out of a hat. Let me know. But if you go by numbers, pick only eleven. We no longer have the original twelve."

A murmuring buzz went around the group as they each stared at the empty seat.

"Unfortunately, Brenda Cornwall will be returning home today. She came to my room with a note explaining that her throat infection had not improved and that it had become more painful. She has arranged to visit her doctor after driving home to New York today.

And, as a very nice gesture on her part, Brenda has donated her full scholarship back to the American History Scholars Program. She had a prepared letter she printed off in the hotel office which she gave to me this morning. The letter explained she clearly didn't need the scholarship money but entered the competition for her own satisfaction. Brenda has requested that next year the program committee expand the number of scholarship recipients from twelve to thirteen with her award money. And I think that is magnanimous on her part and we, the committee, will certainly do that. Now, are there any questions?"

James raised his hand then spoke.

"I think before we all break up for the day, we, ah, the students should vote on presenting in alpha order, or by lottery numbers. So, how many want to do it alphabetically?"

No hands were raised.

"Okay," James said. "I'll write up numbers one to eleven and bring around an empty bowl from which we can all pick. I will pick last. Agreed?"

The students nodded and answered in the affirmative, seemingly impressed with how James was taking control.

The students went back to their breakfast and their socializing.

"So, Tran, what do you have planned for today, our free day?" Becky asked.

"Oh, I'm going over to the Jordan Hall to check it out, and then I'm meeting some relatives to spend the afternoon. What are you going to do?"

"I'm meeting a friend and then we'll decide what to do," Becky said.

"Geez, I'm really upset that Brenda had to leave us unexpectedly. She and I had a lot in common. But she was a sickly girl, I guess."

"Sickly? You mean with her throat infection?"

"Well, that too, but she must have had other problems with health issues."

"Really. Like what kind of health issues?"

"Oh, it's something I saw that first night she sat next to me and we got to know each other, with her jotting notes and my talking. Just before we split up for the night, Brenda bent down to pick up her bag from the floor. When she did so, I noticed a significant scar at the back of her neck."

"Scar? What scar on the back of her neck? Was it a straight surgical incision scar about four inches long with suture dot scars on either side?"

"Yes. Yes, you saw it too! And that's what made me realize the poor girl must have had neck surgery at some time in her life. It's just so sad that she's had a history of health problems, and her being such a talented singer, too."

Becky's thoughts were moving so fast it made her feel dizzy. The room seemed like it was spinning. Tran continued talking, but his voice only echoed in her mind. She couldn't understand a word he spoke. Her breathing was labored as if everything was closing in on her.

Her thoughts rewound to the previous Saturday in that New Haven coffee shop. She recalled the table at Claire's café. When Green Hair had leaned down to pick up her handbag off the floor, she exposed the back of her neck and the thin surgical scar.

That wasn't the rich heiress and singer from Westchester, New York in our scholar group. It was that same freaky bitch who duped me that she was the student from Indiana and then dissed me about being Chinese.

It was Green Hair who was here masquerading as Brenda Cornwall!

CHAPTER SIXTEEN

"Becky, are you all right?" Tran asked. "You seem a little flushed, and all of a sudden you began perspiring."

"Huh? Oh, no, I'm okay. I just think I might get a little fresh air."

"Oh, don't leave yet, Becky! You need to pick your number." It was James approaching with a cereal bowl held high in the air.

Becky stood up, extending her hand into the bowl. She plucked out a piece of paper and unfolded it.

"Which number did you pick, Becky?" Tran asked.

"Oh, I picked the number eight! That's great! It's a lucky symbol in Chinese culture.

"Why is that?" James asked.

"The word for the number 'eight' in Mandarin is 八, bā, which sounds like the shortened word for 'prosperity and good fortune, 發, fā, so it's considered to be good luck!"

She immediately saw the confused expressions on both of the boys' faces and knew it was time for her to leave. She pushed her chair in under the table then gave them her trademark dimpled smile.

"Hey, I gotta go, guys! I have to meet someone. I'll see you later tonight!"

Becky stepped briskly out of the elegant ballroom then double-timed her steps to the elevator bank. When she stepped off at the seventeenth floor, she quickly rounded the corner, nearly bumping into Daniel's mother, Mei Yang. She was outside of room 1790.

Becky decided to speak English with the woman.

"Good morning. I'm going to meet your son today!"

The older, diminutive woman smiled warmly before responding in her accented English.

"That is good. My Daniel is nice son. He's my only son."

"Have you already cleaned this room?" Becky asked, pointing to Room 1790.

"No. But young woman already check out. I go inside room to clean now."

The thought hit Becky quickly. *This could be a great opportunity to snoop around in the emptied room.*

"Oh! I lost an earring and I think I lost it in that room. Several of my friends were in there to take photos. Can I go inside to look for it? "

"Of course! It's empty now."

Mei Yang unlocked the door to Room 1790 and propped it open, enabling Becky to step inside.

Her eyes panned around, searching for any clues about who had stayed inside the room the previous night. Her attention was quickly drawn to the two double beds, which all of the rooms had. Based on the totally disturbed bedding, both beds in this room had been slept in during the night.

Okay, so there were two people staying in this room.

She walked around quickly looking into the trash baskets before Mei Yang emptied them. The one near the base of the cocktail table was not used. But the one near the nightstand had a crumpled piece of paper inside. Becky reached in and plucked out the note paper with the Copley Hotel imprinted on the top. Below that, she saw just one line written down. It was a seven-digit phone number.

When Mei Yang had stepped out of the room to return to her utility cart, Becky slipped the crumpled paper inside her jeans. She checked the basket once again. Something shiny caught her eye. She grabbed a tissue on the nightstand and reached inside picking up the shiny, silver items.

What the hell is this? Oh, my God! It's a set of fake dental braces. They were the same braces worn by Green Hair. *So, even these were part of her disguise. It must have been a deterrent to hide that chipped tooth. She knew I could have picked up on it. The braces covered it up.*

She dropped the tissue with the braces back into the basket.

"You have luck find earring?" Mei Yang asked in broken English as she carried fresh bed sheets and pillowcases into the room.

"No, no luck yet," Becky replied, as she headed into the bathroom.

The bathroom had several damp hotel towels strewn over the tiled floor. She carefully inspected the sink vanity top. There was an empty tube of tanning cream on the vanity. She reflected on the dialogue back in the New Haven coffee shop. Green Hair told her that she used tanning cream both on the theatre stage and off.

She spotted a small residue of a white substance on the counter and on a paper napkin. At first she guessed it might be cocaine. But upon closer inspection, she saw the powder was chunkier in small bits and not very granular. It appeared to be crushed, white pills.

She closed the bathroom door just enough so Mei Yang couldn't see her while she poked inside the trash basket under the granite vanity counter.

She spotted several discarded cotton pads used to wipe off makeup in the wicker basket. Each had a dark green residue on them. She then recalled the last time she was with the group. It was during the session when Samantha spilled hot tea on the imposter's lap. Behind the tinted glasses was a thick coating of green eye shadow makeup. She pulled out another tissue. Underneath the pads was an empty medicine prescription vial. She grabbed the vial and slipped it inside her jeans just before Mei Yang opened the bathroom door to clean inside.

"Nothing here! I'll just look on the carpet and under the bed!" Becky yelled out.

The older woman in her hotel uniform just smiled as she brought clean bath towels into the bathroom.

Becky looked around the decorative floor covering. Her eyes were drawn to the base of the highly-polished, mahogany nightstand next to one of the beds. One of the legs of the modern piece of furniture was visibly damaged, while the other three were unblemished.

Kneeling down on her hands and knees, she inspected the fresh damage. The stained finish on the nightstand's leg was badly chafed, exposing raw wood. The badly marked-up leg had splintered with small pieces of the wood lying on the carpet close to the bed. Based on the gouge marks on the dark-stained wood, it looked as if something was attached to it and had been pulling on the base of the nightstand.

Still down on the floor, she lowered her face to peek under the bed. Although dark, she could still make out an object that had been thrown under the bed.

She extended her arm to reach the object. Her fingers felt the silky material. It felt like smooth strands of hair. Pulling it closer to her, she could see the color of the wig; a bright, honey-blonde.

The wig had belonged to the woman seen entering the two adjacent rooms.

Becky pulled the wig toward her. Before she stood up, her eyes still peered under the bed to the wall beyond. Another door was slightly ajar. She got up slowly as Mrs. Yang still could be heard cleaning the bathroom.

She folded the stolen wig and stuffed it inside her shoulder bag.

As she tiptoed over to the opened door she realized it connected to the adjoining room belonging to Drew Lane. She wondered if the door on his side was unlocked also. Just as she grabbed the doorknob, a loud voice startled her.

"Oh, Becky! You no go in there. Guest still using room," Mei Yang yelled out. "He not check out today—tomorrow, tomorrow he leave!"

"Oh, thank you. I guess my earring isn't here. I'm leaving. Thanks for letting me inside to look around!"

They smiled at one another before Becky slipped by the older woman to return to her own room.

Once inside, she stepped over to the desk drawer and pulled out her personal notebook. She quickly added to the list of questions she had started. She jotted down the findings in Room 1790. Then reaching into her pocket, she pulled out the medical prescription vial. She read the prescription label:

Oxycontin 10mg—Take 1 tablet every four hours or as needed for pain. Will cause severe drowsiness. Must not be taken with alcohol.

She read the name of the prescribing doctor. Underneath was the printed name of the patient, *Drew Lane*. Quickly, she dropped the empty plastic vial into the drawer before closing it.

Washing up in her bathroom, Becky was bothered by the seemingly unconnected events she had recently uncovered. Her thoughts worked feverishly while she dried her hands and face and stepped from the bathroom.

Why would Green Hair, who once tried to pass herself off as Samantha Rawlings from Indiana, now disguise herself as Brenda Cornwall from New York? *If Tran didn't mention that neck scar to me, I never would have thought that girl with the phony throat infection wasn't Brenda.*

A cheeky grin graced Becky's face as she looked into the hotel room mirror.

But the mystery chick hasn't kept anything from me, the teenaged super sleuth and detective from Connecticut. I'm onto her!

Her expression suddenly turned serious.

But...she didn't do this all alone. She found a capable accomplice in Mr. Drew Lane. Professor of American History.

CHAPTER SEVENTEEN

She met Daniel not far from the hotel in Copley Square.

The Boston Public Library was an impressive building with a long history, being the first public lending library in America. Its statues and architecture grabbed the visitor's eye upon stepping up the stairs to the main entrance.

Daniel led Becky on a tour of the hallowed library halls and rooms. The slow walk provided her an opportunity to see the impressive murals, art work, and sculptures. But as they walked slowly around each floor of the building, she told Daniel the full story of what had happened since last Saturday in her hometown in Connecticut, up until the time his mother let her into "Brenda Cornwall's" room on the seventeenth floor that morning.

It was a lot of information for Daniel to absorb, but he listened intently and seemed to understand the sequence of events that led to Becky's angst and frustration as she struggled with such a bizarre mystery.

"There has to be some logical connection with who you call 'Green Hair' and Brenda Cornwall," he said. "And this mystery girl, who evidently also posed as the blonde woman, points to one major question."

"What's that?"

"Where the hell is the real Brenda Cornwall? You said she was mega-rich, from upstate New York. But do we know in fact that she ever made it to the scholarship conference?"

"We don't. She was absent for the first day or so, then Green Hair arrived posing as the sick, non-verbal Brenda, which was part of her cover."

"You're right. The sickness and laryngitis was a ruse. It prevented you from hearing her voice once again. You'd recognize that voice was the same one you heard back in New Haven and would figure something was weird. It would have blown her cover and her impersonation of the wealthy girl from New York."

"But, Daniel, why the hell would she do this? What was the point? What was the motivation to impersonate someone else? It wasn't for the scholarship. In fact, Brooke Gleason told us Brenda wrote a letter requesting her award be donated to some other candidate next year."

"Did you see that letter? Was it handwritten or typed on hotel letterhead?"

"I haven't a clue. Dr. Gleason just told us about it at the breakfast meeting this morning. She was disappointed that Brenda had to return home."

"Well, we have lots to do on this. First, we must find out why the real Brenda Cornwall never showed up at the conference sessions."

"I'm guessing she really was sick and couldn't make it at all. She probably never drove from her home in Westchester, New York to Boston."

"We can find that out by making a quick call to the Cornwall home."

Becky thought about his suggestion. "It's a good place to start. But we must think about a reason to call them. And we might get her parents or, given her wealth and station in life, we're likely to have a house secretary answer our call."

Daniel pondered the situation as they walked by a sign promoting a new exhibit coming to the famous library.

"Hey! What about this? You told me when you searched the room you came across those fake dental braces. What if I make a call to the Cornwall home in my role as a Hotel Security Office staff member? I'll ask whoever answers, if Brenda left behind her dental braces. I will tell them the housekeeping staff found them in her room after she checked out. We know they were fake and never belonged to her, but at least I'll learn if Brenda was even here."

"Great idea! With that one phone call we'll find out if the family knew if she was here in Boston or not! And if she had been here, we'll find out if she returned home early because of her illness."

The two continued walking around the library built in the nineteenth-century. They both admired the historical building's architecture, the art, and the fascinating sculpture work. Few words were spoken until Daniel stopped and faced Becky.

"You know, I think there's one more thing you can see in this library and tell your mom about when you return to Connecticut."

"My mom?"

"You told me she's a law professor and once practiced criminal law, right?"

"Yeah, but believe me, she has enough law books in her den already."

"Follow me into the Rare Book room and you can see something pretty interesting significant to our legal justice system. She would certainly know about the Sacco and Vanzetti case almost a hundred years ago that took place here in Massachusetts."

"Of course! Even I know that it was a historical legal case that later questioned bias and prejudice in a court of law. Some argue that because they were Italian immigrants they never had a fair trial and the judge and jury had already made up their mind. And of course it was guilty!"

"Yeah, racial and ethnic prejudice. Imagine that, eh?"

"So what did you want to show me?"

"Voilà!" Daniel turned then pointed to a display of white plaster death masks of each of the notable convicts, Fernando Nicola Sacco and Bartolomeo Vanzetti. The casts captured their Italian features down to the thick-styled mustaches of the era.

Becky stepped up to the display and read the plaque. Underneath was a sealed container in a transparent case holding the cremated ashes of the two men with questionable and checkered pasts.

"Wow, this exhibit has been here for decades."

"Yup. It's important to the people here that trials must always be fair among everyone regardless of skin color or…the fold in their eyelids."

She responded simply with a grin.

Becky studied the exhibit and took a photo with her cell phone.

After they stepped outside of the iconic landmark, the sunshine had replaced the earlier overcast skies and misty drizzle.

"So when you go home tomorrow, you got a story just for her!"

"Oh, I don't think so. I'm not going home tomorrow."

Daniel turned to face her. "Oh? And why is that?"

"Because, those of us in the Scholars Program can keep our rooms through Sunday. There's no additional charge if we do. So, I'm thinking I might stay here through the weekend."

Daniel didn't try to hide his beaming smile at hearing the unexpected news.

"Aha! I'm thinking perhaps you want to stay in town to figure out what's going on with Green Hair and Brenda Cornwall."

She smiled at him once again without a word as they headed back to the hotel.

"Not just those two women, Daniel."

"Oh? Now that's interesting," he replied playfully with his trademark grin. "Then there must be someone else who you want to learn more about in the next few days."

"That's true! There is someone else I want to know more about. And that man is named Mr. Drew Lane," she responded.

His grin suddenly sank.

Once inside the hotel lobby, Daniel reached for Becky's hand, and held it tightly while he led her into the Hotel Security Office not far from the hotel registration counter. He closed the door behind them. He showed her around the series of small rooms.

"….and when I'm working the night shift and things are slow, I can nap for a while on that couch over there. My boss says it's okay since whatever is seen on monitors is recorded and usually uninteresting or unimportant enough to respond right away."

The dimly lit office had several monitors with live streaming video. Becky recognized the black and white image of the lobby with hotel guests approaching the front desk to check in for the previous weekend.

"Let's make that call to the Cornwall home right away. If we want to solve this puzzle logically, we have to get all of the individual pieces laid out."

"Spoken like a true Computer Scientist," Becky commented with a grin.

They both sat down facing the console unit that held the video monitors. In front of Daniel was a laptop computer.

"Let's first see what we can find out about our Miss Brenda. Here's her registration record that took place early last Sunday morning," Daniel said, while he scrolled through a series of screens.

Several digital data fields about Brenda and her hotel room in green phosphor text seemed neon-bright in the darkened room.

"Is that her signature on the image of the check-in form?"

"Hmm. That's strange. Apparently, she didn't sign in for herself. There's no credit card recorded since the room was pre-assigned to the Scholarship Conference. But it's not her signature on the hotel agreement form." Daniel pointed to the data field.

"I can see that. It was signed by Drew Lane. He signed in for Brenda Cornwall above her name as her proxy. I wonder why that happened."

"We only accept proxy signatures if the guest is underage or is incapacitated in some way, such as physically limited. But let's get to the phone number. That's what we need." His eyes scanned the field of data on the dark screen. "Okay, here it is. Hmm. That's also strange—it's not a New York area code but a Boston area code."

Becky followed Daniel's index finger pointing to the ten digits.

"Yeah. And I know that phone number well. It belongs to Drew."

"So we'll have to look up the Cornwall phone number. But from what you told me and her family wealth, I'm sure it's not listed."

"Wait! I just thought of something. I have a phone number on the paper I pulled out of the room trash."

Becky reached into her blue jeans, and pulled out the crumpled piece of paper. She unfolded it and looked at the number.

"It's a 914 area code. I'm pretty sure that might be upstate New York."

"Let's find out. I'll dial it then put it on speaker phone."

A man's articulate voice answered the call.

"You have reached the Cornwall residence. This is Frederick speaking. With whom am I speaking?"

"Oh, ah, Frederick, hello. This is Daniel Yang at the Copley Hotel Security office in Boston. I am just inquiring about a personal item we found in Brenda Cornwall's room. Apparently, she left it behind after she checked out. May I speak with her?"

"Checked out? She's supposed to check out tomorrow. She's not here at this time."

"Ah, that may have been her plan, however, I am told she had a relapse of her throat infection and decided to return early."

"Throat infection? She has no throat infection. Who is this? Mr. and Mrs. Cornwall received a text message from her just a few hours ago. Brenda texts home each day from Boston. According to her parents, she was doing fine and would call home when she begins her drive back tomorrow—not today. In fact, we don't expect her home until late Friday afternoon. So, I'm sorry, Mr. Yang, but you have some erroneous information."

"Oh, I am sorry for the confusion."

"But what item did your staff find that might belong to Brenda?"

"Oh, my notes say it was dental braces or a retainer of some sort."

"Dental…ah, you have the wrong room. Brenda has nothing like that!"

Daniel's eyes searched Becky's face for a signal as to how to respond.

Becky grabbed a pen then scribbled on a piece of paper. *Drop it!*

"I'm very sorry to have bothered you, Frederick. Someone must have written down the wrong hotel room number where that item was found."

"Well, Mr. Yang, that is obvious. Brenda doesn't wear nor ever did wear dental braces of any type. So you do have some bad information. Good luck with your pursuit."

"And, again, I am so sorry to bother you. Thank you, sir."

The next sound over the speaker was the Cornwall house phone hanging up.

Daniel exhaled loudly, relieved that the tense phone call had ended.

"So, what did we just learn?" Becky asked, before she stood up and paced around the Security Office.

"Well, we know for sure now that the real Brenda never made it to the conference program. And we confirmed those fake braces were part of Green Hair's disguise, masquerading as Brenda Cornwall," Daniel added.

"Yeah. She had to conceal her teeth with fake braces because I might recognize her teeth or the smile I had seen in New Haven. See, I'm the only one who met up with Green Hair."

"Not true. Brenda also must have met up with her at one time or another."

"What did you think about Brenda texting back home each day?"

"Well, anyone who got hold of Brenda's cell phone could send texts to the Cornwall home. The parents would never know it didn't come from their daughter. Do you think Brenda's all right? I mean, do you think she ran away or…"

"Or was kidnapped?" Becky finished his question.

"But, Becky, we really don't know that."

"Of course! But what's the motive behind this weird, freakin' charade?"

"I don't know, but I was just thinking about something. Of all the kids who came here for the conference, Brenda was by far the wealthiest. Most of the kids who won the scholarship really needed the cash to help pay for their four years of college. I bet most of their parents couldn't write a check for tuition, room, board and all other expenses. Isn't that true?"

Becky sat down once again and turned in the swivel chair to face Daniel.

"Yeah, perhaps that's true for most student scholars, but not for my parents," Becky commented.

Daniel grinned before his next question. "Are you bragging that your family is a member of the one percent demographics…that you're part of the so-called privileged class?"

"No, no. Not at all. But my college education expenses would never be a financial burden on my parents. I'm fortunate because they both hold high-income jobs. And…Green Hair had done research on my mother. That weird chick discovered how Mom had defended some front-page, high-profile court cases many years ago."

"Okay, and…this is important, why?"

Becky simply stared into space before she answered. "Because I now know why Green Hair came to New Haven to meet me, yours truly, Becky Bing."

CHAPTER EIGHTEEN

"What do you mean?" Daniel asked with a surprised expression.

"When we first talked in that coffee shop, she told me she had already done research on my family. She knew my father is a well-known orthopedic surgeon with his advanced techniques for treating bone cancer going global."

"Wow! I had no idea. But why the hell would she do any background checking about you and your family?"

"Because…I now know that I was her original mark. You see, I was the original intended kidnap victim coming to this conference."

"Becky….I don't…"

"I told you she was pissed and totally blown away when I pulled off my sunglasses. She almost croaked when she saw that I'm Chinese-American. Now I know why. She assumed I was a Caucasian because she had seen a picture of my mom on the net. See, my mother is white with blonde hair and blue eyes. My father however, is Chinese."

"Your mom is white with blonde hair and blue eyes?"

"I'm special. I'm adopted, but, hey, let's not get off topic. When Green Hair saw me, she totally deflated. She immediately knew it would be a risk to try to impersonate an Asian girl. She had a sudden meltdown. It was then that she borrowed my phone and made her call to someone who I later discovered was one of the program coordinators, Mr. Drew Lane."

"And he's the one in Room 1792, right?"

"Right! So Drew and Green Hair must have agreed to call off the plan to use me as their kidnap victim. Even as a good actress, it was too risky for her to impersonate me, a Chinese-American. It was especially dangerous if someone here in New England knew me or had a photo of me. Her cover would be immediately blown. Green Hair rudely told me she was shocked to find I was Chinese. She said something like, 'I thought your last name was like the American Bing cherry.'"

The expression on Daniel's face became more serious. His golden complexion drained into a dull pale color.

"Holy crap! This little mystery is now getting way more serious than I had thought. I was thinking maybe it was some sort of sick high school prank, but nothing so sinister as kidnapping."

"Some pieces are beginning to fall into place, Daniel! Green Hair and Drew knew my family had money and that I'd be a good kidnap victim in a ransom deal. But Green Hair couldn't disguise herself."

"But wait, we don't know if any kidnapping was involved. This is still only speculation. We still haven't found Brenda. Maybe she just never showed up here. And right now, we can't prove your theory."

"We can't prove it…yet!"

"But, Becky, there hasn't been a threat or mention of ransom money. So we still don't know for sure if the motivation is kidnapping."

Just then, a tall African-American man with greying hair, wearing a blue suit and silk, striped tie stepped into the office.

"Hello, Daniel! I didn't know you were already in today."

Daniel and Becky stood up to greet the gentleman.

"Oh, Mike! This is Becky Bing. I was just showing her around. Becky, this is my supervisor, Mike Stone."

The two shook hands, exchanging cordial smiles.

"It's nice to meet you, Miss Bing! Maybe you'll want a career in security and surveillance in the future after Daniel shows you the ropes around here. Hey, I was just going across the street to Dunkin Donuts for a coffee. Can I get you guys anything? It's my treat."

They each politely declined the offer before the distinguished-looking gentleman stepped out of the office.

"Hey, you've got a really cool boss!"

"Yeah, he's one of the reasons I like working here. But I was just thinking about something. If Brenda Cornwall did check into the hotel on Sunday morning, even if Drew signed her registration, she'd be on our surveillance video."

"Great, can you restore the vid from Sunday?"

As Daniel accessed a library of video recordings, Becky looked at the several monitors in and out of the hotel. They included the ballrooms, lobby, and each floor of the prestigious landmark in Boston. There were cameras outside in the connected parking garage at the rear of the building.

"Okay, it's loaded for that time of check-in. Let's take a look!"

They both watched the recorded view of the lobby. At that time of day there was much activity near the registration desk. Lines of people were queued, some checking out, and others checking in early.

"Hey, isn't that Drew at the desk now, but without his goatee?" Daniel asked.

He slowed the recording to single frames. The surveillance camera had been set up behind the front desk. It had a slight downward angle. But the faces of guests were clear with the lens nearly straight on them.

"Yep. That's Drew all right. He wore that same leather jacket in the New Haven train station. I'm positive about that."

Daniel let the video speed up and continued to narrate. "Okay, so he signs in and is now chatting with Elyse, our front desk clerk. She works the Sunday morning shift. She's a senior at Boston University. Hey, look! He's pointing to someone behind him."

"It's someone in a wheelchair. Look, she has a bandana on her head and she's wearing sunglasses!"

"So we can't identify her. But if Drew is pointing to her and he just signed in Brenda Cornwall, we can safely believe it is because she is in the wheelchair."

"And so that's how they snuck our victim into the hotel," Becky commented.

"And look at her body in that chair. She's slumped to one side, probably drugged. You told me you found an empty vial of narcotic pills in her assigned room."

"Yeah. And I think they gave the meds while she was imprisoned in Room 1792."

Daniel scratched his head as his expression grew more serious. "Becky, we gotta go to the police with this. There's nothing we can do now. We can just tell the cops what we have discovered and let them take over."

Becky suddenly became pensive, staring at nothing before checking her watch.

"I think we might do that too, but not now. All we have today is a series of circumstances that may or may not have led to a kidnapping. So far, no crime has been committed that we can confirm. So until we can prove it we really can't go to the police."

"It's true. But let's remember what…ah, Frederick told us on my phone call. He didn't indicate in any way that Brenda was in any trouble…especially nothing about a kidnapping."

For a brief period, they both became quiet; deep in their own thoughts.

"Hey, Daniel, are you going to be working here at the hotel tonight?"

"Yeah. I have to archive some tapes and then install some software to one of the computers in the administration office. Why?"

"Oh, I was just wondering if you'd want to come to the final dinner tonight in the Abigail Adams room. We can invite guests to join us for dinner and then listen to our scholarship-winning presentations."

"Becky, I'd love to be there tonight as your guest! I look forward to it."

"Great! I'll get your name on the invitees list right now."

This time, it was Daniel who leaned in toward Becky and gave her a brief but tender kiss on the lips.

"Thanks!" Becky replied when she opened her eyes.

The smile stayed with her when she stood up to leave the darkened Security Office.

Up in Room 1775, Becky laid out her outfit for the evening on the bed. She had packed a red, above the knee, silk dress with a Mandarin-styled collar. The festive outfit would top patent-leather black pumps with small, red bows. She'd planned to sweep her hair back with a thin, red-velvet headband that matched the color of her dress.

Later, while she was enjoying a hot shower, her thoughts ran free but with more questions than answers.

What if Green Hair is Drew Lane's girlfriend and accomplice? If Brenda is gone from Room 1792, did they relocate her into another room? Perhaps it's a room on another floor? If my theory is true, how long will Brenda be kept captive?

And if my theory is not true, I have made an ass of myself with Daniel Yang. And that's something I don't want to do.

I wonder if I could get accepted to MIT? That's stupid; it's so close to Harvard, we could still see each other.

While toweling off, she mused at how she and Daniel had met through his mother, the hotel housekeeper. His warm smile and sensitivity made her grin as she wrapped the large towel around her naked body.

But as she stepped out of the bathroom, her thoughts switched to Jake who was now flying out to Colorado with his mother.

Jake's my first real boyfriend. These past six months have been great with him. But he's right. We're both going away to college soon and shouldn't let our relationship hold us down. We'll always be good friends and I hope we'll always stay in touch.

She stretched out on her bed then picked up her notes for the night. She had spent a lot of time on it, but now underlined those words she wanted to emphasize during her five-minute presentation.

Just as she closed her eyes to drift off to sleep a loud rapping on the door startled her from her dreamy state.

The loud male voice came in from the hallway with another sequence of rapping.

"Becky, are you in there, it's Drew Lane."

"Ah, yeah. What is it?"

"I'm just checking on those students who decided to stay through the weekend. I assumed you're going back to Connecticut, but I need an exact head count to give the hotel registration desk."

Becky peeked through the security peep lens.

"I decided I'm not going back to Connecticut tomorrow. I'll be staying on, Drew."

A short pause hung in the air.

"You will? I mean, are you sure?"

She saw a frown furl on his face through the tiny security lens.

Is he disappointed that I'll be hanging around through the weekend? And if so, why?

"Ah, yeah. I'm sure. I'll be leaving on Sunday."

"Hmm. Okay. Thanks."

She watched through the tiny peep hole as he turned abruptly, heading down the hall toward his own room.

The Abigail Adams room was filled with all of the conference attendees and many secondary school history teachers, college professors, and their guests. There was a non-alcoholic "social hour" for everyone to mingle and meet before the dinner program began.

Becky and Daniel approached Samantha who was chatting with Lynn. Each held a cold drink and a small plate of appetizers. She introduced Daniel to them before he headed off to get drinks for Becky and himself.

"Hey guys! Are you excited about our last night here?"

"Yeah, Beck. I was thinking about staying the weekend, but I really want to get back home. My little brother misses me and wants to hear all about his sister's first trip away from home," Samantha replied.

Becky smiled at her new friend. "Oh, does Drew know that you won't be staying? I mean, did he stop by your room and ask you about that?"

"Huh? No. He never stopped by my room to ask me," Samantha answered.

"He never stopped by my room to ask me, either," Lynn interjected. "I wish to hell he did stop by my room. I'd give him something he'd never forget and make him want to see me in Santa Fe real soon!"

The three girls giggled at Lynn's remark. The crowd seemed to be growing with invited guests dressed in jackets and ties, the women in attractive dresses and outfits. It was now jammed near the Social Hour end of the ballroom.

"Hey, I need to get some more shrimp cocktail! Be right back," Lynn said as she drifted away.

James Blackstone's southern accent drawled from behind them. "Hey, I'm getting some more appetizers. Can I get you ladies something?"

"Ah, no thanks, James. But you are truly a southern gentleman," said Becky.

James nodded his head with a smile and then spoke with an exaggerated drawl and demeanor. "Why, thank you, Miss Becky. It's always my profound pleasure to serve the most beautiful ladies at dinner parties."

Samantha pushed him away laughing. "James, you're over-the-top now!"

"Hey, James, did Drew ask you about staying on through the weekend?" Becky asked.

"Nope, haven't seen Drew all day." He looked over toward the table and then brought back the drawl. "Oh, I must leave you two ladies. I believe I see a damsel in distress that I might be of service to by the bar."

Becky looked at Samantha, who didn't understand the real purpose of her question about Drew.

"Becky, I have your address and cell number. And I'll connect with you on Facebook as soon as I get back to Indiana. My bus leaves real early in the morning."

"Great. And tell Glen I'll do another duet with him over Skype any time he wants."

"You know, Becky, in a way I'll be glad to get back home. I mean, I liked meeting you and the conference was great, but this whole thing about that spooky girl with green hair using my name really scared the crap out of me. But now I really think it was some weird prank that never worked. Anyway, it's out of my mind now and I'm sure you'll forget about it soon too!"

"Oh yeah. It's already out of my mind too," she lied. "Oh, here comes Lynn. She's carrying appetizers. Now it's my turn to get some goodies."

She looked through the crowded guests standing in groups and spotted Daniel coming toward her with two plastic cups of iced ginger ale. She led him through the line, filling a plate for the two of them with some cheeses, grapes, and a chilled shrimp cocktail.

They found an open space with a small table to set down their drinks.

"This is quite the dinner party! I actually recognize some of the people here. There are some professors from MIT milling about and I saw a couple of well-known authors here."

"And I'm so glad you came! By the way, Drew Lane knocked on my door after I left you."

"And what did he want?"

"He told me he needed to know before tonight's dinner which students were staying at the hotel through the weekend. He seemed surprised and a little disturbed when I told him I was staying on."

"Really? That's interesting. But I suppose the front desk needs to know which students will still be in their rooms through Sunday morning."

Becky stared at him. "Except…I've since learned that I was the only student he asked."

CHAPTER NINETEEN

The evening's formal program began with students being asked to occupy the front dining tables. The head table looked festive with large vases of colorful flowers. There were name tags for each student at two tables giving them assigned seating.

The hotel staff encouraged invited guests to find seating in the other cloth-draped tables to enjoy socializing with other invitees during the dinner program.

As soon as everyone was seated, Brooke Gleason stepped up to the podium. This evening the program facilitator looked stunning in a green silk dress with scoop neckline revealing a modest view of cleavage. Her earrings matched the emerald color. The antique silver necklace added to the ensemble and complimented her shiny, black hair neatly coiffed for the evening. After getting everyone's attention and adjusting the microphone, she introduced herself and began her welcome address to the audience of over one hundred people.

"I want to thank all of you for attending the annual American History Scholarship Awards Dinner this evening. We are all so happy you are here to meet the student winners who come from across our nation, and to listen to their papers which will be presented after dinner is served.

"There is a printed program near your dinner plates and we intend to keep on schedule as much as possible. I do want to acknowledge some of the well-known personalities who are with us tonight and…."

Becky's attention drifted as she turned her head to look at the full tables behind her. She spotted Daniel wearing his suit jacket and tie, seated next to a slender, black woman. The two seemed to be engaged in an animated conversation.

She quickly reached for her small, black leather bag and pulled out her cell, placing it in her lap. Without annoying anyone, she sent a text to Daniel.

Hey! Pay attention to the speaker! You seem chatty with the pretty woman to your left!

Her attention then swung back to Dr. Brooke Gleason.

"The hotel wait staff is bringing salads to your tables now and you won't hear from me again until dessert is being served. So, enjoy your meal with those around you and make new friends!"

Tran Nguyen sat directly across from Becky. Next to him was an empty seat.

"Hey, Tran, is the name tag next to you for Brenda Cornwall?"

"Yeah, it is. It's a shame I didn't get to see her before she left. I decided to stay on through the weekend and had hoped we could attend the Boston Pops together at Symphony Hall. But I'm pissed because I wanted to connect with her after the conference. It's too bad I didn't ask her for her home phone number up in Westchester."

"Hmm. Did you ask others if they got it from her?"

"Well, I've asked a few others but it seems nobody knows what it is. I might try the hotel's front desk staff."

A mental seed suddenly germinated in Becky's fertile mind.

Just before she was about to respond to Tran, a woman's head lowered down between her and Lynn. It was Brooke Gleason.

"I'm just on my way to the powder room but wanted to stop by and thank all of you for such a nice week up here at the conference. And I want to wish you all luck in your presentations tonight!"

"Oh, thank you, Dr. Gleason. It's been a fun week!" Becky responded.

Lynn swiveled in her chair to face the attractive professor. "Oh, Dr. Gleason, I love the scent you're wearing tonight. What is it?"

"Oh, it's something I picked up on Cape Cod this past summer. I think it's only sold locally. It's called 'Nantucket Breeze.' I put it on often, even with my casual outfits."

"I really like it," Lynn commented with a smile. "The name fits, like a salty breeze blowing up onto the beach."

"Yes. It's very nice…and it's so distinctive," Becky added.

"Why, thanks, girls! I have some in my bag here if you'd like to try it."

"Ooh, I'd love to put some on," Lynn responded.

Brooke reached into her leather shoulder bag and pulled out an atomizer of the perfume. A blue and white image of a sailboat was on the label. She handed it to Lynn.

Lynn squirted the bottle toward her neck and upper chest area then returned the small bottle to the professor.

"Thanks," she said with a smile.

The pert Dr. Brooke Gleason sashayed away from the two girls, gracefully moving around to speak with all of the students seated at both tables. She also wished them luck on their presentations before she exited the ballroom.

Becky and the other students chatted, feeling the excitement in the air, anticipating their presentations. But she always kept a curious eye on Daniel Yang, seated next to the attractive woman at a table toward the rear of the hotel ballroom.

She also looked at the head table. Drew Lane's focus was aimed at the student scholars' table. His piercing stare with serious expression made her feel uncomfortable.

Why did that bastard come to only my room and ask if I was staying longer?

Is he suspicious that I might be onto him and Green Hair working together?

Is that guy who is so good-looking and academically bent really capable of ambushing a student?

Later, when dessert, coffee, and tea were served, Dr. Gleason returned to the podium. She thanked the hotel staff then segued into the program explaining how the order of presenters was established with students picking random numbers.

"And I'm proud to say that this year's scholarship winners have provided the most convincing factual history based on facts and data they have researched. As you know, these brief presentations tonight are only a synopsis of each student's detailed submission that dispute, negate, or minimize what has been printed in our American History textbooks for years. They, too, have uncovered some truths that we all want to hear about.

As social scientists in this room, all of us are mandated to uncover truths, and report information that provides the integrity with our teaching the subject of American History. Tonight, you'll hear about distortions of truth in several historical events that include: the bombing of Pearl Harbor, the hidden architects of the Vietnam Conflict, some disturbing facts behind the Industrial Revolution, and how the most famous poem by Henry Wadsworth Longfellow, "Paul Revere's Ride," is riddled with myth and misleading lines absorbed into accepted fact in our school textbooks throughout the nation.

I hope you enjoy the presentations and get to meet the scholars after the program. And now I want to bring up our first scholar, from Franklin, Michigan, Mr. George Norris."

The presentations were brief; most keeping to within the five minutes of their allotted time. Their presented synopses provided some insight into the scholar's paper that enabled them to come to the conference and receive the monetary scholarship award.

After Lynn's talk on the Military Joints Chief of Staff's secret role during the Vietnam Conflict, she ended with a smile, sat down, and eyed Becky sitting next to her.

"Well, now that I have that over with, I just have one more mission before I head back home to New Mexico."

Becky gave Lynn a quizzical look, taking in the scent of Nantucket Breeze, earlier sprayed on her body.

"You have another mission? What's that, Lynn?"

"I want to spend some one-on-one time with Drew Lane. You know, I just feel I should thank him for what he did for me." She paused while focusing on the young man sitting at the head table. Then she turned to face her friend. "But as I told you, I want to thank him…my way."

Becky couldn't hold back her girlish giggle, having to cover her mouth with her cupped hand. Lynn did the same.

Soon, it was the eighth student's turn in sequence; lucky number eight in Chinese lore. Becky approached the mahogany podium and microphone.

As a preamble to her talk she explained how the famous Longfellow poem, "Paul Revere's Ride," detailed in its rhythmic way, a perception of what might have occurred at midnight on April 18, 1775. Then she underscored Brooke's introduction; how the content of the poetry had quickly become adopted into history text books, distorting the facts of the first night of the American Revolutionary War and the legendary hero, Paul Revere.

Becky looked out at the audience.

This crowd is almost falling asleep with listening to talks of bloody and depressing historic wars. I'm gonna shake it up a bit. I'll wake this audience up with a little humor. I think I'll ad lib a bit. What the hell have I got to lose?

"First of all, it is public knowledge how Sarah Palin was totally wrong in her comments about Paul Revere's ride. But she's only a politician. And I doubt she'll ever return to Boston!"

The crowd chuckled at her comment.

"When the two-year Governor of Alaska visited this fine city, she publicly misstated the facts. But, Sarah's not alone. Many of our text book publishers have done likewise. Those American History books are still used in our school districts throughout the nation.

I believe most of you know Paul Revere is credited with making that legendary ride in April 1775. But he was not alone; in fact, he had about forty or so companion riders with him that night to ride west to the towns of Lexington and Concord. Of course they are never mentioned in the books and never got credit for their critical role. Only good ol' Paul did. My research uncovered that Revere had a great publicity agent…himself!"

The audience reacted with more loud laughter, loosened up by the levity of Becky's presentation. Out of the corner of her eye she saw Daniel step closer to the podium and take photos with his cell.

"Now, I have two questions for all of you. Nobody ever seems to think about the answer to this and it's rarely mentioned in Paul Revere's historical ride. Like so many facts that became overshadowed by the poetic verse, my first question is this: although Revere had heard street rumors that King George's militia would attack soon, my question is…who actually told him for certain it was going to be the night of April eighteenth? Does anybody know who that person was?"

Several arms quickly went up in the air among the audience of history professors and graduate students.

"I know!"

"Yes, ma'am."

A slender, salt and pepper-haired woman spoke out.

"I do. It was Doctor Joseph Warren, a local and respected surgeon."

"Correct! And he told Revere to alert John Hancock and Sam Adams out toward the Lexington and Concord way. But my next question is; who told Doctor Warren that the war would really begin on that night? Who told him that…to use a lyric of singer Rod Stewart, 'Tonight's the Night?'"

More audience chuckles as Becky's eyes panned the full audience seated under the dimmed chandelier lighting. But, as she expected, no hand went up in the air.

"Okay. I'll tell you the name of the confidential informant. Her name was Margaret Kemble, or more accurately, as the wife of British General Thomas Gage, her name was Margaret Kemble Gage. This native New England woman didn't want her military husband to begin a war that would 'slaughter her own countrymen'. So, when she learned from her husband, the respected General, how the attack would definitely take place on that evening, she secretly told Warren who immediately summoned Revere to his office.

"But it was soon discovered that the brave and sensible Margaret Kemble Gage was the confidential informant to Warren and the revolutionary patriots. Her husband, upon learning this, immediately sent her back to his home in England. Unfortunately, we never heard again about this courageous and unsung heroine.

So Paul Revere became the legendary hero, getting all of the heroic credit in the poetic verse of Longfellow's work. The poem and emulating textbooks state that Revere moved swiftly and smoothly on his mission. He did not.

Once he rowed to the opposite side of the Charles River, to mount a specially-selected, swift mare given to him by another local horseman, Revere discovered he forgot something; his spurs."

The crowd once again broke out in laughter. Becky then continued.

"So another trip back had to be made, where Revere's assistants rowed dangerously across the Charles, returning to the North End of Boston to get his spurs. Then this crew bravely rowed back once again to the other side of the Charles to bring the famous silversmith his forgotten spurs. Then the hero was ready to make history. The rest is sketchy at best, but we know Revere never made it to Concord. He stopped at a pub, had a few pints, and later was captured during his famous ride, but later released. He owed a debt of thanks to his redcoat captors.

Revere gave one account of his ride soon after the event. But days later he re-wrote it, giving himself all the credit for the ride, making him a hero. And we all know it was the revised copy that Longfellow used for his poem.

I enjoyed researching this American History project and hope you get to read my entire research paper. I also must recommend the detailed information outlined in the book, *Paul Revere's Ride*, by David

Hackett Fisher, published by Oxford University Press in 1994."

Becky smiled, knowing she had just hit a home run with the audience and faculty. The audience gave her the loudest applause of the evening. She nodded with a smile then picked up her notes and stepped away from the podium.

The audience continued to applaud loudly until she reached her chair and sat down.

CHAPTER TWENTY

The remainder of the student talks were brief and the program concluded on time at nine o'clock.

Brooke Gleason had a few closing remarks and explained how one of the high school scholars, Brenda Cornwall, had to leave unexpectedly because of illness. She also informed the crowd that Brenda's research paper would still be published in the annual booklet along with the eleven other scholarly materials.

As the event broke up, many from the audience approached the students to congratulate them on their performances. Becky attracted the lion's share of the well-wishers, with many college faculty asking her to consider their college for her future plans. Two graduate students from Harvard enthusiastically talked to her about spending time with them and encouraged her to attend the Ivy League school the next fall.

"Becky, I have to say goodbye now," Samantha Rawlings said. Her arms opened wide to hug her friend.

"Oh, why now?" Becky asked as the two embraced.

"I've got a seven o'clock bus trip back home in the morning. I have to be at the Greyhound terminal by six-thirty."

Becky put on a friendly and exaggerated pouting face to show her melancholy.

"That's too bad. But I have your email and cell number. I'll call you later this week."

"Yes! And please Facebook me. I know Glen will want to be your friend as well!"

As she watched her friend leave with the others from the hotel ballroom, she felt a personal sigh of relief that the naïve girl from Indiana wasn't staying the weekend. She didn't want her becoming upset again knowing there were serious loose ends with the mystery of Green Hair, Drew Lane, and Brenda Cornwall.

Daniel approached her with a warm smile on his face.

"Congratulations, Becky! You're a rock star. You put on quite the performance! Well done!"

"Thanks, but the only thing I want to do now is get out of this dress and back into my blue jeans."

"Okay. Meet me downstairs in the Security Office later. I'm the only one in there tonight and I have something important I want to show you."

Becky called her parents from her room and told them how her speech went. She also explained that the dinner program was the last formal meeting and that the Friday morning breakfast session was merely optional.

The Bings understood why she wanted to stay through the weekend to enjoy the city of Boston and its college student atmosphere.

Minutes later, she was on the elevator going down to the lobby, now dressed in casual clothes. She slipped into the Security Office unnoticed.

"Okay, Daniel, so you really got my curiosity. What is it that you want to show me that's so important?"

Seated inside the dimly lit video monitor room, Daniel tapped the computer keyboard. A black and white surveillance film came up showing the hotel lobby.

"Now, watch. There is no activity in the lobby until I fast forward some frames."

Becky watched as she saw Drew Lane pushing a wheelchair by the registration desk. Again the woman being wheeled in the chair couldn't be identified. She had the same bandana and sun glasses she wore when Drew had checked her in the previous Sunday morning.

"Hmm, so he pushes her wheelchair straight toward the front entrance."

"Right! Now watch this. I switched to see what the camera over the front door recorded," Daniel said.

The camera showed Daniel pushing her to the curb where a dark BMW sedan was waiting. A woman with blonde hair or wig, sunglasses, and long, dark raincoat got out from the driver's seat and helped Drew get the girl into the back seat. Then the driver got back inside the front seat and drove away.

"Now, watch!" Daniel said. "I switched cameras to the one located back inside the lobby. Watch what happens. Drew is coming back inside."

They both focused on the young man now returning inside pushing an empty wheelchair. They watched each frame click by as he parked the wheelchair near the front desk then stepped away, heading toward the elevators.

"Hmm. So we know they put her in a car and whisked her away. They picked a time when absolutely nobody was around. And we know the driver was wearing that same blonde wig and sunglasses, and at nighttime, no less! By the way, what time did this take place?" Becky asked.

"Look. The digital time is at the lower right corner of each frame. It was exactly midnight when he put her into the car."

"So they decided to put that poor girl on her own midnight ride."

"Now we know she's definitely gone from the hotel. But we don't know where that midnight ride took her."

"Well, if she left here at midnight last night, she'd certainly be home in Westchester by now if that's where they were taking her. It's only about a three-hour drive from Boston."

"But her driver may have made stops along the way, especially if she really wasn't feeling well. She may have had to make some stops."

"True. And the Cornwalls' house manager, ah…Frederick, said they weren't expecting her back home until tomorrow, Friday afternoon."

"Some things still bug me from what you've told me, Beck."

"Me too! Like where do you think Drew Lane fits into all of this? Is Green Hair his girlfriend, and are the two of them accomplices or are they doing the dirty work for somebody else?"

"Well, Drew is a problem. And I don't have an answer for what he's up to in this whole thing."

"Hey, is there any way you can tell me when Drew checks out tomorrow morning?"

"Sure. There will be all kinds of computer system updates as soon as he checks out. It triggers the housekeeping database so they can do their work. I can put a flag on his database record for his room number and be alerted when he's out of there."

"And do you think we can get your mom to open the door for us after he's out and before she cleans the room?"

Daniel laughed. "So you like to use all of the Yang family in solving your mysteries, eh?"

Becky chuckled and rolled her wheeled office chair towards his. Her legs interleaved with his longer legs.

"No! That's not true," she responded, leaning into him. She gently placed her hands on his face and then gave him a tender, but prolonged kiss.

After Daniel composed himself, he continued his questioning.

"But you do want to get into Drew Lane's room right after he checks out. Isn't that right?"

"I do. I won't be but a couple of minutes and may not find anything, but I really need to check out his room for any clues."

"Well, my mother's not working at the hotel tomorrow, so she can't help you out."

"Oh."

A confident grin curled his lips.

"But, since I am the Security guy, I can get into any of the rooms if there is some security issue." He paused. "Maybe I'll need to check out Room 1792's key-card reader at the door, while you perhaps slip inside and look around."

Becky's face beamed with a glowing smile.

"Daniel! Thanks for doing this!"

"Hey, we can still make the late, late movie at the Boston Common theatre. Are you up for it?"

The two hustled out to the hotel lobby. They held hands while they pushed through the heavy, revolving entrance door.

"Now there are lots of films to choose from. The only request I have is that we don't see some 'chick-flick'. Is that okay with you?"

Becky turned toward him as they walked briskly through the center of Boston.

"Fair enough! As long as we don't see some action-adventure, blood and guts, explosions. I really want to see a good film."

"Like what?"

"Like, you know, like a good mystery that's difficult to solve!"

They both laughed as they waited for the light to change at the crosswalk.

Behind them, and out of sight, was a black BMW sedan driving slowly up to the traffic light. The only thing noticeable on the driver was the short haircut, so that it was impossible to tell if it was a man or woman behind the wheel.

CHAPTER TWENTY-ONE

After her city jog-run on a cool Friday morning, Becky vacillated about attending the final Scholars' breakfast session. But waiting for the elevator, she decided she had already said her goodbyes and would much rather enjoy a long, hot shower and then call Daniel after his early morning classes.

In the steaming shower, her thoughts drifted back to her first real boyfriend, Jake. She knew he was now back in Colorado, visiting the Air Force Academy and taking a tour of the campus.

I really hope his visit and Air Force Academy interview went well. Although it hurts that our young romance is drawing to an end, I know Jake will find happiness at the college he wanted. And he so loved his dad, who would be so proud of him attending the academy. And of course, his mom will be back in her hometown and with her mountain hiking friends.

Her thoughts continued, realizing the pain of breaking up had been minimized since she met Daniel Yang. Although he was two years older than she, the handsome college sophomore was already becoming special in her life. In just a few days, they both discovered how they had much more in common than just their Asian heritage.

Daniel was a gentleman and respected her space. Already he had shown support by helping her with the bizarre mystery that had followed her from New Haven to the conference in Boston. They liked the same music, the same movies, and both were ambitious students who wanted to learn as much as they possibly could.

While she wrapped a large hotel bath towel around her naked body, her thoughts shifted to getting accepted into Harvard. And having Daniel nearby as her friend would make the transition from her small Connecticut town up to Cambridge, Massachusetts that much easier.

She texted her mom once again to check in and tell her she'd be touring more of Boston with her new friend.

I know Mom will understand when I tell her all about Daniel. I really want her and Dad to meet him.

Her cell rang while she was pulling on her blue jeans and sweater.

"Hey, Daniel, how was class this morning?"

"Huh? Oh, it was fine. Listen, ah…can you come meet me right away? I just got in at the Security Office. Something's come up."

"Oh? What is it?"

"When I got in this morning, I had a handwritten phone call message from one of the hotel staff. It was left on my desk. The note said I must return a very important phone call—as soon as possible."

Silence hung in the air before Becky cleared her throat.

"Really? Who was the call from?"

"The handwritten note just has the caller's first name. It was from…Frederick."

Becky's face became a confused frown. It was a name she'd never expected to hear again.

"Hmm. That's interesting. Is it a New York area code phone number?"

"It's the same area code, but it's not the same telephone number as the Cornwall residence, where we called the other day. It might be his cell."

"Hey, can you come up here to make that call? I wouldn't want your boss to come into the office while you're talking to this, ah...Frederick."

Becky quickly dressed and bushed her hair before Daniel's knock at her door.

"Hey, Beck! Just before coming up here I got a database electronic message that I had set up. Drew Lane has already checked out of his room."

"He did? Can you open the door to his room now that it's empty?"

"Yep. Let's go."

The two stepped slowly along the carpeted hallway looking around to make sure nobody was watching. They stopped in front of Room 1792 and Daniel used his master key card to open the door. After determining nobody was around, they both slipped inside. Daniel closed the door.

One of the beds was still made up neatly, while the other had bedcovers and sheets tangled into a twisted, disheveled state.

So, only one bed was used in this room. The other untouched, unlike Room 1790.

While Daniel feigned looking at the door lock for some problem, Becky scooted around looking everywhere for clues.

The bathroom was clean with nothing in the small trash basket. There was nothing left behind on top of either the desk or the bureau.

Becky moved quickly with her eyes searching for something that might help her learn more. But the room appeared to be clean and free of any clues.

She walked over to the pillows and picked them up, thinking there might be something left underneath them. As she did so, she was suddenly shocked at what she discovered. It wasn't anything she saw. It was a scent that she smelled. She brought the pillow closer to her nose to reaffirm the scent.

The unique scent was like the salty breeze blowing up onto the sandy beach.

I know that scent! It's Nantucket Breeze! It's the same scent that Brooke Gleason gave to Lynn. And Lynn put it on last night.

Becky dropped the pillows and then her eyes shot down to the small trash basket near the bed. There was a square, foil-package ripped open lying at the bottom of the receptacle. She knew without examining it what the wrapper had contained.

So, Lynn carried out her amorous mission with Drew Lane as she told me she would. Man, that chick was determined to sleep with her "hot guy" before she returned home to New Mexico—and by God, it looks like she accomplished that mission!

Her thoughts were interrupted by Daniel calling out. His voice was low; just above a whisper.

"Hey, Beck! Are you almost finished? We can't be in here too long."

"Yeah, I'm all set here. There's nothing left behind that will tell me more about Drew." She turned toward the door. "That I need to know," she added.

Back inside Room 1775, Daniel sat on one bed, while Becky sat on the one she used at night.

"Okay, so I have this new cell number and I have to call Frederick back. I'll call and put it on speaker phone again so you can listen."

"Wait! Let me get a notepad. I think he's going to tell us something important."

Daniel made the call from his own cell phone.

"Hello, Frederick, I'm returning your call."

"Daniel, I need to talk with you. And I really need your help. Something has happened since you called me. Brenda has been kidnapped! But…please don't call the police or FBI. Her parents are so frightened that something might happen to their beloved daughter. They want to handle this on their own."

"How did you find out she's been kidnapped?"

"There was a phone call last night. The caller's voice was muffled and he or she only wanted to speak with Mr. Cornwall. They warned that if he didn't follow directions, they may never see Brenda again. Mr. Cornwall talked to the caller and listened to the demands."

"Demands?"

"Yes. Ransom money. Evidently, you were onto something. Brenda didn't stay for the entire Scholar's Program but probably left early, driving back here to New York. According to the caller, they ambushed her along the Massachusetts Turnpike when she stopped at a service area for coffee and to refill her gas tank."

"So…where is she now? Did they tell you where they have her now?"

"No. But they told Mr. Cornwall that he should prepare for instructions where they would meet to make the transfer. You know, where they'll exchange Brenda for the ransom money."

"Did they say what the ransom amount would be?"

"Yes. Five million dollars is the amount. Mr. Cornwall is already visiting some of his banks to get the money."

"God, this is awful, Frederick. I don't know what I can do to help."

"First, and above all, don't tell the police. That is critical! If her captor finds that the police are involved he promised he'd immediately kill her. Second, since you were onto something where she left the hotel early, I want you to think of anything that might lead me to learn who the kidnapper might be. I will work on my own to identify this bastard even if it's after Brenda is returned safely here to Westchester."

"Frederick, I think I can help, but it involves a friend of mine who was part of the Scholarship Program. She was onto some bizarre things involving Brenda and told me about it. I can speak with her to find out more."

"Yes, yes, of course! Do that and whatever else it takes. But understand, no police or FBI can get involved or poor Brenda will be killed and left somewhere."

"I understand. Should I contact you at this same number?"

"Yes. It's my personal cell. Texting might be better. The Cornwall family has no idea who you are or even that I contacted you."

"Okay. And this cell is the best number to contact me, when you need to."

"Call me back after you have met with this young woman. Let me know if you learn anything. We have to move quickly. I presume Mr. Cornwall will deliver the five million dollars after a drop-off point is agreed upon. Then it's only a matter of time before the kidnapper leaves the country."

Daniel disconnected the phone and immediately fell backwards onto the top of the bed. He spoke to Becky still sitting on the other bed while he stared up at the hotel room ceiling.

"My God! This is getting real freakin' serious now, Becky." He placed both his hands over his face, covering his eyes. "Your theory that this, this Green Hair chick who impersonated Brenda was involved in a possible kidnapping is now a proven fact!"

Becky stood up, moved over to the other bed, and lay down next to Daniel. She too, faced the ceiling.

"Yeah. And think about it. If I weren't Chinese and so difficult to impersonate, that would be my family getting the phone call looking for ransom money. And it would be me being held with a death sentence over my head."

Daniel turned to face her. His hand moved gently to her forehead, brushing away her black hair.

"I can tell you something. I am so glad you're Chinese, Becky."

She turned to face him, staring into his coal-black eyes.

They shared a soft and gentle kiss and warm embrace before sitting up.

"Let's go somewhere. I think we can both use some fresh air," Becky suggested.

CHAPTER TWENTY-TWO

The cool Saturday morning had warmed up since Becky's early run but they decided a walking tour of the city was out of the question now that they were drawn deeply into a capital crime; the kidnapping of the wealthy Brenda Cornwall.

They headed for the Boston Common and found an empty bench where they could talk and still do some people-watching of the city's pedestrians.

"So we know Green Hair and Drew Lane are our suspects, and we know how much money they want to return Brenda to safety; five million," said Becky. "But you and I know something Frederick doesn't. Brenda didn't drive her car along the 'Mass Pike' on her way to New York. In fact, she probably is still somewhere here in Boston."

"Perhaps they took her to another hotel either in Boston or somewhere in the suburbs. It'd be too risky to keep her inside the Copley," said Daniel. "And, besides, Drew had to check out since he was a facilitator of the Scholars' program."

"For all we know, he could be headed back to Columbia University. Perhaps his part of the kidnap job was done. Remember, Frederick told you he couldn't tell if the caller's muffled voice was male or female."

"Yeah, so Blondie, who you believe to also be Green Hair, is still our mystery woman. It would help if we could get her identified. This is going to be real tricky without asking the police to take the case over."

"We can't risk endangering Brenda's life," said Becky. "And I'm sure Mr. Cornwall will come up with the five million and do what the kidnappers dictate."

"In a way, that might be best, if Brenda is returned safely."

"Daniel, I just had an idea, I had seen that chick with the blonde wig step into the lobby bar at the Copley. She must have ordered a drink from the bartender or from a cocktail waitress."

"So you think we should go inside Periwinkle's and ask around?"

"No. I was just thinking about playing them with their own game. You know, using a disguise."

"Huh?" Daniel asked.

"What if I dress up to look like the mystery blonde? You know, with sunglasses, maybe a trench coat like hers and some lipstick. She used tanning cream, but I won't need it. And I already have the same blonde wig I scored from under the bed. I'll put on some heels for added height. Then I can walk into the bar, see if any of the staff or patrons recognize me as the blonde and get them to talk with me."

"It's worth a shot."

"Good, let's do it!"

"I said it's worth a shot, but Beck, it can be risky. Somebody might figure out it's you and it could turn dangerous."

"I know that. You go find me a light raincoat in the hotel lost and found or from one of the female staff. I have the sunglasses and the blonde wig." She paused then smiled. "Hey, maybe you'll like me better as a blonde."

Daniel laughed.

She jumped up, reached out for his hands, and pulled him up from the park bench.

Later, up in Room 1775, Becky put the final touches to the blonde wig; spraying it into a style similar to the woman in Room 1790. Daniel had just dropped off a trench coat he'd discovered in the lost and found department.

Before leaving the room, she slipped on her sunglasses, covering most of her face. She put on a pair of high heels to get her elevation close to the height of Green Hair.

Just as she stepped around the corner of the seventeenth floor in high heels, she almost bumped head on into Daniel's mother, Mei Yang.

Mrs. Yang smiled at her with a cheerful, "good morning."

The housekeeping woman obviously didn't know it was Becky Bing behind the disguise.

That's a good sign. The disguise is working.

Becky imitated the blonde's gait in the heels as she stepped into the entrance to Periwinkle's.

She chose a stool at one side of the bar, providing a good view of all the patrons at tables and the entire bar.

The voice of the middle-aged, balding bartender startled her as he approached her. He stood face to face with her.

"Hey, Marty! Haven't seen you in a few days! Can I make you your usual, a pomegranate martini?"

Becky forced a fake cough, thinking quickly.

"Uh, I've a little cold," she replied, forcing a nasally tone in her voice. "I want just a ginger ale, please."

Before he nodded and turned to the soda dispenser, she saw his hotel nametag on his maroon vest, "Jack."

When he brought the iced drink to her with a cocktail napkin he had an apologetic tone.

"You know, Marty, I felt bad about asking you for ID the first time you came in here. You had that youthful look, and the ABC, ah, the Alcoholic

Beverage Commission, would close us down in a minute if we served an underage person. But happily, your driver's license proved me wrong."

"Ah, don't worry about it, Jack. Happens all the time," Becky answered.

"Hope you feel better!"

She nursed her iced drink for a few minutes while looking around the intimate bar and lounge restaurant, but nobody else seemed to recognize her. After dropping a five dollar bill on the bar, she waved to Jack and left.

Back in her room, she slipped out of her disguise and immediately texted Daniel with her update.

Her first name is Marty. Jack, the bartender, had checked her ID, a driver's license. Can you question him as a potential security case without giving him any details, before he leaves for the day?

Daniel responded to her message quickly.

I'm on it.

Within a few minutes she had another text reply from Daniel. But it wasn't about Jack the bartender.

Becky read the screen message.

I just heard again from Frederick. The kidnapper called the Cornwalls' home again. He was only told the drop-off for the ransom money would be someplace in the city of Boston. They'll call again with further details. Frederick wants to talk with you and me later tonight @ 8. Still nervous and warns us about not going to the police.

Becky didn't respond to the text, knowing he was on a mission. She was proud of herself that she'd teased out a little information with her own skillful impersonation of the blonde at Periwinkle's. Now she was hopeful Daniel would find out more about this imposter chick. But she'd have to wait to hear back from him.

With some time on her hands, she called home to check in with her mother and dad.

Later, she sat at the hotel room desk to review her notes hidden inside the desk drawer. She then got up and walked to the window on the seventeenth floor. She thought about the mystery while peering out the window at the Boston skyline. Her eyes focused on the steeple of the Old North Church.

My gut tells me Green Hair and the blonde woman, Marty whoever, are one and the same. And I know she also played the role of Brenda Cornwall here at the conference. I never would have guessed that until Tran told me about the surgical scar on the back of her neck. She had pale skin here but when I met her in New Haven she looked well-tanned with the help of the tanning cream. It all fits in. She's a good actress, can change her voice, and loved putting on theatrical makeup and costumes.

But I still don't know why or how she hooked up with Drew. They must have met some time ago and planned the kidnapping. Maybe they are a couple.

But now I understand a lot of why I'm into this mystery. If I weren't Chinese, my parents would be getting those calls now about coming to Boston to drop off the ransom money.

Ha, if this Marty is Drew's girlfriend, she'd be pissed to know how Lynn Faulkner had her sights on him and left the scent of "Nantucket Breeze" on his pillowcase last night.

Her cell rang, disrupting her thoughts.

"I talked to Jack at Periwinkle's about Marty," Daniel said.

"And?"

"He remembered checking her driver's license to validate her age. He told me it was a Massachusetts license. He remembered her hometown since he grew up not far from her."

"Really? Where's that?"

"Quincy."

"And where is Quincy located?"

"It's on the South Shore about ten miles from here. It has a huge Asian American community; Chinese, Vietnamese, Cambodian, what have you. I actually have a lot of friends from school who live in Quincy."

"Hmm. Did Jack, the bartender, remember Marty's last name?"

"Yeah, he did. He told me it was easy to remember because it's a common name."

Becky picked up a pencil. "Okay. So, what's her last name?"

"Lane."

CHAPTER TWENTY-THREE

"Lane? Holy crap! But…is she Drew's wife or…"

Daniel cut her off. "Becky, we don't know the relationship and I clearly couldn't ask Jack. But at least we know who she is and now can do some research. Unfortunately, we have to do it on our own. We can't go to the cops."

"I know. We have to move fast, especially if Frederick is getting a call at eight tonight."

"Look, I've got some things to do downstairs. I'll be back before noon. Why don't you research this Marty Lane from Quincy and I'll catch up with you later."

Becky got to work on her laptop looking for anyone named Martha Lane from Quincy, Massachusetts. The internet profile of the city confirmed what Daniel had told her. The city was often called "Chinatown South" for its influx of Asian American citizens now living south of Boston's own Chinatown district.

She quickly found the listed name of a 'Martha Lane' residing at the Colonial Apartments. Then she called Information to get the phone number.

I've got to call this number to verify that it's her. But I'm sure as hell not using my personal cell phone or the phone in this room.

She took the elevator down to the hotel lobby and slipped inside the Security Office.

On her way in she bumped into Daniel's boss, Mike Stone.

"Hey, Becky! Oh, Daniel's not in right now."

"Yes, I know, but he's on his way here from school. Do you mind if I wait for him in the office?"

"Ah, sure. I don't mind at all. He'll be here soon. I'm on my way to the hotel kitchen area to look into a little problem. The front desk will page me if I'm needed."

Becky went directly into the darkened room with the surveillance monitors and closed the door behind her. She sat down and paused, thinking of a story to use if she should make contact.

She picked up the hotel phone and dialed the number of the apartment belonging to Martha Lane.

"Hello."

Becky immediately recognized the voice belonging to Green Hair. She then began her mentally rehearsed script. But first, she squeezed her nose to disguise her own voice, giving it a nasal tone.

"Hello, is this Martha Lane?"

"Who's this?"

"Oh, this is the Security Office at the Copley Hotel calling. Your name was provided to us by the bartender at Periwinkle's Lounge. There was an incident here at the hotel and his name was brought up as a person of interest. He's looking for people who can vouch that he was tending the bar at the time of the incident. Your name came up. He said you were a patron in the bar and you can verify his being there at the time. I'm just asking if you might be home in a couple of hours to answer a few questions from the detective on the case. Will you be at this address this evening?"

"Huh? I don't know what the hell you're talking about. I only went into that bar twice."

"Yes, but the Boston Police want to ask you to verify the time you were in there. You'll be contacted later. We appreciate your cooperation."

"Huh? Yeah, what the hell! Unfortunately, I'll be here all night."

Becky hung up the phone and exhaled a sigh of relief.

Just then, the door opened. It was Daniel.

"Is your car in the garage?" Becky asked.

"Yep."

"C'mon. We're taking a ride to the Colonial Apartments in North Quincy. I'll explain why while you drive there."

The traffic was heavy on this Friday afternoon along the Southeast Expressway leading out of Boston. But it provided time for Becky to tell Daniel why they were headed to the Colonial Apartments.

"So what do we do when we get there?"

"I'm not sure yet, but according to her telephone directory listing, she's in apartment 413. So, it must be on the fourth floor."

"But, Beck, are you thinking that is where they took Brenda Cornwall until the ransom drop off takes place?"

"Maybe. Who knows?"

"If she's being held hostage inside Apartment 413, what the hell are we gonna do? We can't just force ourselves inside and pull Brenda out of there."

"Daniel, there is no *we*. When Green Hair, ah…Marty, opens the door and sees my face, she'll just slam the door and lock it."

"So what's the plan?"

"So, you're going to have to knock on that door and talk to Marty by yourself."

The inside of Daniel's sedan became silent as the highway traffic began to lighten up.

"Geez, and I thought my database design tests were nerve-racking! Those are a piece of cake compared to doing this."

Becky turned and smiled at him then grabbed his hand, raised it up to her mouth, and kissed it.

"Do you think any of your friends might live in the Colonial Apartments?"

Daniel pulled out his cell phone. "That's a good question. Let me find out. I can call someone."

After contacting a friend and a brief conversation, he turned to tell Becky that two of his classmates lived in the suburban apartment complex. He accelerated the sedan as the traffic thinned.

"Gary Chan is a good friend of mine and also lives on the fourth floor. It's apartment 421. He's an advanced communications network nerd, and such a cool guy. There's another girl, Cindy Wang, who I just met in my thermal dynamics class this semester. She lives on the second floor, apartment 252."

Becky smiled as her mind began working on a plan.

Within minutes they had pulled into the parking lot of the Colonial Apartments.

"Let's just walk around and get a layout of the place. If anyone asks, we're looking for a friend who is showing us an apartment to rent."

The two ambled up through the main entrance while the sun was beginning its descent across the western sky.

They took the elevator and stopped at the second floor and walked confidently along the corridor before returning to the elevator. This time they went to the fourth floor. Slowly, they approached the door with the number 413.

But what they saw surprised them. Taped to the door was a handwritten message on yellow legal-sized paper:

Leaving area soon! Apartment is available on October 1st. Inquire within or call the telephone number below.

At the bottom of the sheet was a series of tear-off tabs with the phone number. Becky immediately pulled one off then kept walking toward the end of the corridor.

When they reached the end, they took the exit door and stepped down into the cement and steel stairwell.

"This is interesting, Beck. It looks like she's dumping her apartment. Clearly she won't need it if she comes into a pile of money."

"Yeah, especially if it's ransom money to the tune of five mil'."

"Check out this number! This is not the same number I called from the hotel. I called the land line number to her place. And I know it's not Drew's number. I'd remember it if it were. This has to be Marty's cell."

"Okay!" Daniel responded. "Now we need to refine our plan. Look, there's a lot of Asians renting in this building. Not that I want to, but what if I knock on her door, asking more about the rent or sublease? If she's alone and not keeping Brenda in there, she'll let me in to look around."

"Great idea! I'll wait here."

Daniel turned to leave, but Becky reached out and grabbed his arm. She pulled him closer to her and put her arms around his shoulders. She gave him a kiss that lasted longer than either of them expected.

"What's that for?" Daniel asked with a smile.

"That's just for…for good luck! Be careful."

Becky waited in the stairwell. When a young couple jogged up the stairs, she put her head down, pulled out her cell, and feigned talking on the device until they passed by.

After nearly ten minutes, Daniel returned.

"How'd it go?"

They both descended the cement steps speaking softly to avoid the echo.

"Good! I got in. And she showed me around. Nothing special inside, so we know Brenda isn't in there. There was nothing left in the apartment, except a large suitcase and a small flight bag already packed and ready to go."

They reached the first floor then stepped briskly toward Daniel's car.

"Hey, before you go any further, tell me what she looked like."

"Oh, kinda weird. She had very short hair not much longer than a buzz cut. The color was sort of a mousy brown. She had plain hazel eyes, and her skin complexion was pale. She wore a plain old t-shirt from a Coldplay concert and belted blue jeans."

"And she showed you around the apartment?"

"Yeah, it smelled like cigarette smoke in there."

"Oh, that's right. I had forgotten that. Green Hair…ah, Marty is a smoker. Parliaments is her brand of choice as I recall. She lit up when we walked in New Haven. She told me she only smokes when she's stressed out."

"Yeah. Well, the place was very plain; nothing on the walls, because she's moving. I didn't spend much time after I walked around quickly. There was a laptop still opened up on top of her bed. I wanted to get out of there because I was nervous."

"I understand. But did she seem nervous, letting a strange man come into her place?"

"No. She had protection."

"Protection?"

"Oh, I forgot to mention that one little thing. There was this butt handle of a handgun shoved into her jeans. It was obvious she wanted me to know she had a gun."

Becky looked at him as the slid into his front seat. Her mouth dropped open, and then she spoke.

"Oh."

CHAPTER TWENTY-FOUR

As Daniel turned the key in the ignition, he spotted another young Asian man walking by the front hood of his car. He was headed toward the entrance to the apartment building.

"Hey, there's Gary!" Daniel said as he rolled down his window.

"Who?" Becky said squinting at the man reaching for the front door.

"Hey, Gary. It's Daniel. Come meet my friend, Becky!"

The tall Asian man had long, black hair tied back in a ponytail. He smiled when he recognized Daniel in the driver's seat then stepped to the side of the car.

"Hey, Daniel! What's up? What are you doing here?"

Daniel first introduced Becky then lied that they were just looking at apartments to rent for a friend.

Gary invited them up to his apartment for a cup of tea.

When they entered the small place, they were overwhelmed by the number of computers, file servers, and monitors throughout the living room. There seemed to be electronics and technical manuals everywhere. Gary moved hardware devices from the sofa to the floor for his two guests to sit down.

The three chatted while Gary prepared tea and put out a plate of sesame cookies.

"So, check it out! There's a place available right here on this floor. Did you see the sign on the door?" Gary asked.

"Yeah. In fact, that's really why we came here."

Daniel and Becky told a story of how the tenant in that apartment might be involved with something serious. But they told it in such a way as to not divulge any of the sensitive facts and the kidnapping of Brenda Cornwall.

"Oh, that's right! Daniel, I forgot you're the security guy at the Copley. No, I never saw the chick. Seems she's never around when I'm here. But with my lifestyle and weird hours, that's not unusual. Hey, do you know her cell phone number?"

Becky perked up. "As a matter of fact, Gary, we do now. It was on the tear-off on her door."

"Oh, good! Maybe I can help you out a bit. I won't do anything illegal, and I can't wiretap to hear any conversations, but I can tell you when she makes calls and where they go to and come from. My coordinates will be within a few city blocks. My hardware and software is not overly sophisticated, but is definitely accurate."

Becky shot up from the sofa. "Can you show us who she's been contacting in the area?"

"Like I said, I can show you who she's been contacting anywhere on planet earth within a city block or two. Come, I'll show you."

Gary stepped over to a desk with a laptop camouflaged in a mountain of manuals. He cleared off the text books then turned to Becky for the phone number.

After keying in Marty's cell phone number, the communications expert launched a software program, complete with graphics and a string of numerical digits.

"See these numbers? It's finding the GPS coordinates of each call. I put in a parameter of all calls to and from that cell from the last forty-eight hours."

The program completed with a list of nearly a dozen numbers scrolling up on the computer screen.

"Okay. Now, I take the coordinates and feed them into a graphical map application. The program applies the file and soon an aerial view from GOOGLE earth fills the screen with a bird's eye view."

"That is soooo freakin' neat, Gary!" Daniel commented.

"Okay, the location finder is now zooming into this part of the country, which is no surprise. Here, we can zoom in further and look! We're closing into the city of Boston and now…now we're into the North End section of town. Ah! See it stops there." He pointed to a few blocks of buildings. "I can't tell which house address, but it's definitely in the North End within these few streets. I'd think it is somewhere near the general vicinity of Margaret Street and Sheafe Street. That makes sense since that area has a lot of condos and apartments."

"Gary, can you print out this bird's eye view of streets?" asked Becky.

"Sure."

He printed off the screen image and handed it to Becky.

"Wow. That's really cool!" Daniel said.

"See the cell number on the lower left hand corner. That's the number your girl in this apartment building was contacting. Do you want me to look up who has this cell phone number?"

"Thanks, Gary. But I already know who owns that cell number," Becky replied.

On the return trip to the Copley Hotel, Daniel turned to Becky.

"It's too bad we couldn't get an exact location in the North End, but if you want to start canvassing those few blocks, we might somehow get lucky. Besides, I could go for some good Italian food. That's where you can get the best and most awesome Italian food!"

"Hmm. That's funny. That's exactly what our tour guide told us when we visited that area on our first conference Boston tour. He told us that if we ever want great Italian food, we should return there to any of the restaurants in that section of town."

"Oh, yeah. Hey, who was your tour guide?"

"It's the same guy who has the cell phone that Marty called. Drew Lane."

While approaching the city of Boston, Daniel got a call. He looked at the number then his eyes swiveled quickly to Becky.

"It's Frederick."

Becky looked at her watch.

Daniel listened to Frederick, not saying much except for intermittent "Yups" and "Uh-huhs" before finishing the call.

He pulled into the Copley parking garage and parked in the sections designated for employees only.

"So, what did Frederick have to say? Did the kidnapper call early with the directions for the ransom drop off?" Becky asked.

"No. That call is still scheduled for eight o'clock tonight. But Mr. Cornwall won't be taking the call. He was rushed to the hospital. He just had a serious heart attack."

"Oh my God! The stress these bastards put him through caused the heart attack, I'm sure. Is he gonna be all right?"

"Too early to tell. Frederick told me he has to tell the kidnappers when they call that it will be he who handles the matter for the Cornwall family. Mrs. Cornwall is by her husband's side at the hospital."

"My God! That poor man! He's really got a lot on his plate with this crap. I wonder if this will screw things up with the kidnappers."

"Damn! I wish we could go to the police right now. They'd know how to handle this. I'm really out of my wheelhouse on this and I think you are too!"

"We can't, Daniel. If anything went wrong and Brenda got hurt…or worse, we'd never forgive ourselves. And we could never face the Cornwall family or…or Frederick. We were told to leave the cops out of it and we have to obey that request."

"I know…I know, but damn, I don't have any idea how to find Brenda before the ransom drop off takes place."

Becky interrupted. "Meet me up in my room in a few minutes. I have an idea!"

When Becky opened the door to Room 1775, something caught her eye on top of the bedspread cover on top of her made-up bed. She walked over to it and slowly picked up the note. It was clearly printed in pencil, however, it was unsigned. She stared at the words.

Becky,

Have a safe drive back to Connecticut.

She held the note at arm's length, staring at the carefully printed text.

Who wrote this? Maybe it was Mei Yang. She's the only one who could get into the room while I was out. But it doesn't look like her writing.

She set the note down onto the nightstand and started up her laptop, browsing for a particular website.

When she opened the door for Daniel, she led him to the note then sat down on the bed.

"What do you think? This was on my bed when I got back. Could it have been your mother wishing me a safe trip back home?"

"For one thing, that's not my mother's handwriting, or rather, printing. She's not working today. And she'd never know how to spell Connecticut correctly with the silent letter 'c'. She hardly knows English."

"That scares me. Who the hell was in my room?"

"Maybe somebody asked the housekeeper to leave it for you on the bed."

Daniel handed the note back to her, passing it by her face.

"So, what are you thinking?"

"Ah, I don't know. Maybe it's nothing. But I was just thinking how I never told anyone I drove my car from Connecticut to here. There are only two people who could know I drove to Boston."

"Who?"

"Marty Lane when she was known as Green Hair in New Haven, and her buddy, Drew Lane."

"Hmm. That is strange. So what's your plan? You wanted me up here to do some planning."

"Yeah. Help me figure out the streets on this aerial view of the North End. I was just pulling up the streets that Gary showed us at his apartment."

"Okay, you want us to walk around there and snoop a little? We could ask people if they've seen Marty or Drew Lane in the area. We might find out where he's staying and that's probably where Brenda is hidden."

"That's it. But we gotta work fast. Frederick's getting his call soon."

The two kept looking at the buildings in the area Gary Chan had identified as the spot where the phone calls had taken place. Daniel moved the cursor around and jotted down some residence buildings.

"Hey, wait a second. How far is this neighborhood away from Salem Street?" Becky asked.

"Oh, it's real close. Watch, I'll hover over it."

Their faces touched as they both eyed the arrow cursor moving up and down Salem Street in the North End. Suddenly, Becky's hand grabbed his wrist on the touchpad and stopped it from moving.

Daniel looked at her with a confused expression.

"Daniel!"

"What?"

"I know where they're hiding Brenda Cornwall."

CHAPTER TWENTY-FIVE

"Where? Where do you think she is?"

"She is in the Old North Church on Salem Street."

"But, how…where…?"

"Down in the cellar where the human bones are stored in all those crypts from hundreds of years ago."

"I was at the Old North Church as a kid on a tour, but I never went down into the basement where the bones are stored."

"Well, a certain young man worked a deal to live there free of charge after building a small apartment. He told the Tourist Bureau how he'd be the night watchman for the church and protect the landmark in case anyone broke in."

"And does that certain young man go by the name of Drew Lane?"

"Yes, yes. Daniel, I know I'm right. It makes sense to me. Drew is keeping Brenda Cornwall hidden in the bowels of the famous Christ Church more commonly known as the Old North Church."

The anxious excitement of the moment was sharply interrupted by the sound of Daniel's ring tone.

Becky checked her watch.

"Oh, it's just about eight o'clock!"

Becky listened while the conversation took place.

"Yes, Frederick. Okay. We may have some information, but we're not sure. Yes, there are no police involved. Hmm. That's interesting. Becky and I will check it out. I will."

Daniel disconnected and stared at Becky for a moment without speaking.

"What's happening?" Becky asked.

"Frederick told me he now has the ransom money. It was immediately delivered to him. And Mr. Cornwall is improving but will be in the hospital for several days. But the most important thing he told me is the drop-off point for the ransom."

"Where is it?"

"Near the Paul Revere statue; you know, close to the Old North Church."

"Oh, my God! Now I'm sure Brenda's hidden in the cellar apartment of that building!"

"Frederick told me he must deliver the cash in a large, black plastic trash bag. He's been directed to dump the bag into a brand new trash barrel that will be placed not far from the Revere statue. According to the kidnapper, the trash barrel will be easy to identify with two bright orange stickers on the cover. Then he was told to step away and head toward the base of the statue to wait."

"Wow, this exchange plan has been thoroughly thought out by my pals from the Scholar's Conference. Or, should I say, the imposter actress and the hypocrite professor. But, whatever I call them doesn't matter. They're both kidnappers and if they get caught they will be in prison for a long time."

Daniel continued.

"So Drew will probably take the money from the trash barrel and take it to a car or back inside the church apartment after Frederick drives off. I bet Marty will escort Brenda out from the church after Drew validates that all the money is in there."

"Yeah, and they can keep an eye on Frederick standing by the statue at the same time. So if there's any wrong move, or appearance of any cops, they could take a shot at him. He'd be a sitting duck near the statue. And Marty would still have Brenda."

"And we already know that Marty is packing a gun. Maybe Drew has one, too," said Daniel. "Frederick will get more details, but he knows the exact time of the ransom drop off."

"What time is that?"

"It'll be Sunday at midnight."

Becky grinned.

"So, there will be one more midnight ride for good ol' Paul Revere."

"Yeah, but this time, Paul will be all alone in the dark of night. He won't be surrounded by forty or so friends," said Daniel.

Becky smiled at her new boyfriend, leaned into him, and gently planted her lips on his with a tender kiss. "So, you really did pay attention to my presentation the other night."

"Of course!"

A tight embrace followed. When they separated, Becky made an audible sigh then lowered her face into her opened hands.

"We have to get over to the North End early tomorrow. We have to plan something and we don't have much time."

"I know."

"I understand why they picked Sunday night for the ransom exchange. It's the quietest night in any city—especially at midnight. Everybody's in bed getting sleep for work or school on Monday morning."

"Hey, Beck! Speaking of school on Monday morning, aren't you leaving here tomorrow morning, Sunday? You have to be back for your Monday classes."

"Yeah, but there are no classes this Monday in Connecticut. It's Rosh Hashanah, the Jewish New Year. All public schools are closed in my district. I take it that holiday isn't observed here in Boston?"

"No, I guess, individual states' rights make for a patch-quilt nation of policies, politics, and religion."

"That's too deep for me right now. I'm gonna call my folks and tell them that something's come up."

"And something has come up. My mother wants you over to our house for a meal. Since you're around tomorrow, that'd be perfect. She was thinking dinner, but with all this going on, now I think we should have you come to our house for lunch."

"That's sweet. I'd love to have lunch with you and your mom. But we have to get to work right after we eat. The clock is ticking and we have lots to do."

"I'm starting right now with a plan," Daniel said, as he picked up Becky's spiral notebook. "The Old North Church still has religious services each Sunday morning, but the tours begin at one o'clock and continue until five before the church officially closes."

"Look, I know where the key ring is kept to get us downstairs. I saw Drew reach for it when he gave us the student tour. It's in an altar desk drawer. Somehow, I've got to get at that without anyone seeing me."

"Okay, let's work on that! And we have to plan how to communicate after you go inside the church."

"Me?" Becky asked.

"Well, yeah, you know where this hidden basement apartment is located."

"For now, let's not think me, let's think we," Becky replied with a smile.

Daniel kicked off his shoes and lay back on the pillows of the bed, notebook in hand.

"Hey, I'm going to order room service. I can't think when I'm hungry," Becky said.

"Sounds like a good idea! I'm starved too!"

Becky opened the room service menu with a variety of snack foods from the hotel kitchen. "I'm thinking after we get our plan together, we can order a movie."

Daniel smiled at the suggestion.

"Great! But let's hold off until I've gone downstairs to the Security Office. I still have to do the weekly system file back-ups for the hotel's databases and the camera surveillance files."

"Of course, but we have to talk about strategy and potential scenarios that could happen tomorrow night and how we'd handle each one."

"Like?"

"We have to get inside the church in the afternoon, sneak downstairs, and verify if Brenda is in there. When we get into the apartment, we must confirm Brenda is hidden there.. And, if she is, which I believe is true, we won't know if Brenda is alone or if Drew is staying in there with her."

"Or…Drew and Marty. They both could be in there prepping for tomorrow night."

"So, after we get downstairs, we have to draw whoever is in there out of the apartment."

Daniel became quiet then made a suggestion.

"That cellar must be well over three hundred years old, Becky. But if it got renovated and Drew's bachelor pad was accepted by the town fathers of Boston, it had to have been inspected."

"Inspected for what?"

"You know—his new electrical work, plumbing, heating, and all the stuff."

"Okay. But where are you going with this inspection stuff?"

"The building inspector would have to make sure any and all smoke alarms or detectors are properly installed and up to code down there in the cellar. Especially since the area was partially converted from being a basement to living space."

"Ah. I see what you mean. If we could set off the smoke alarm while they're in the apartment we'd draw them out of the apartment."

"Yep. But we'd have to hide somewhere to see who it is that runs out of the apartment to find out why the alarm went off."

"Okay. I remember there's lot of nooks and crannies down there in that creepy cellar. It's very dark down there, I think on purpose. It adds to the atmosphere when tourists go down into the crypts. You know, musty and dirty like any cellar. So, we must find a spot to hide first. Better bring a small flashlight."

"I'll get one."

"I don't think there is a cellar door. But maybe there is one for an escape route."

"Wait, before we get ahead of ourselves, we must figure out a way we can get the smoke alarm to go off to draw them out of there," Daniel said, interrupting his note-taking. "That's not so hard, but we can't let Drew and Marty become suspicious of how we do it. Or, they'll come around looking and sure as hell, they'd find us!"

Becky became pensive for a few moments. Then suddenly her eyes widened.

"Hey! I got that covered, my friend! Just make a note that we must stop by a store to buy a pack of cigarettes sometime tomorrow morning. And by the way, make that Parliament cigarettes."

"Check!"

"Now, after we determine who is in there, we have to figure out a way to get Brenda out of there. And, we have to get her out before midnight."

"And then we call the police?" Daniel asked hopefully.

"And then we call the police."

Daniel got up from the bed and slipped on his shoes. Before heading down to the first floor Security Office, they both ordered from the room service menu.

When she was alone, Becky called her mom to tell her about coming home one day later, on Monday. She also told her how Daniel's mother had invited her over for Sunday lunch and she was looking forward to it. She closed the call by promising to call home again the next day.

After washing up in the bathroom and drying her face, her cell rang.

"What's up, Daniel?"

"Listen, I just got a call from Frederick while I was doing my work here in the office. I told him I was busy for a while and suggested he talk with you. I told him you'd bring him up to date about everything. I should be back up in less than an hour. I'll give you his cell number."

Becky thought about what she would share with Frederick. She knew she'd have to reassure him that the police or FBI hadn't been contacted. She dialed his cell phone.

"Frederick, this is Becky. Becky Bing."

She told him about what had transpired in the last several hours and why she thought Brenda was being held hostage in the basement of the historic and legendary church.

He expressed his heartfelt concern about the safety of Brenda.

"I'm also concerned about the safety of you and Daniel, Becky," he said. "But I am so afraid if I called in the police or FBI, there may be worse consequences."

"Frederick, what time will you be in Boston?"

"I'm coming early to find my way around with my car's GPS. So I should be in the North End of the city around nine or ten o'clock. I was told where to park my car, not far from the Paul Revere statue. Then I'm to carry the money bag to the trash barrel just before midnight. After doing that, I wait by the statue for Brenda's release."

"Good. If we can, we'd like to help her escape before the arranged money drop. But that remains to be seen. In any case, as soon as you have Brenda in your custody, then and only then will we call police."

"Good, because I can't. One of the kidnappers will first approach me. He will take my cell, verify that it's mine and confiscate it. Since they think I'm doing this by myself, they have no idea you are involved. So, Becky, you and Daniel can call right after the transfer."

"Text me or Daniel as soon as you arrive in the North End."

"Will do."

"Then you must do one more important thing. I want you to erase all phone numbers and text messages before you hand over your cell. If not, they will know we're working together on this and could screw up the whole thing."

"Good thinking. I will certainly do that," Frederick replied.

"Oh, I have one question. Do you have a current photo of Brenda? And if so can you send it to me?"

"Ah…sure. I'll email it to you and Daniel. Why do you need a photo of her?"

"Because…I've never seen or met Brenda!"

CHAPTER TWENTY-SIX

The next morning, Daniel worked in the Security Office while waiting for Becky. Around ten in the morning she came down and the two met in the lobby. "I'm ready. But hey, I never asked where you and your mom lived."

Daniel smiled. "Oh, we're lucky. We have a nice place down on Huntington Avenue, near Northeastern University. It's close to everything in the heart of the city."

"Good, so getting to the North End shouldn't take long."

"But something else has been bothering me about our plan," Daniel said.

"Like what? What's bothering you?"

"It's simple. They, or at least Marty Lane, own a gun. I know that because I saw it. We, on the other hand have nothing. It's a very dangerous line we're going to cross, once we make our way down into the basement of the Old North Church."

"I know. I've thought about that, too."

The drive from the hotel to the Yang apartment was less than fifteen minutes. But it took a little longer when Becky wanted to stop at a florist to pick up a colorful bouquet for Mei Yang.

Mrs. Yang welcomed Becky into her second floor apartment with her arms opened wide to embrace her warmly.

Becky gave the older woman the fragrant bouquet along with her youthful, dimpled smile. Soon the three of them were seated around the table for a delightful meal of both Asian and American dishes.

The chatter was pleasant. After the meal Becky helped Mrs. Yang with the dishes.

Daniel kept busy texting and taking calls on his phone while he paced around the apartment.

At three o'clock, the two students left the apartment with Becky thanking Mei Yang, the hotel housekeeper-cupid, for a delightful luncheon.

On the drive to the North End, Daniel took out his cell and handed it to Becky. The screen was filled with a young, attractive woman.

"Recognize this photo?"

"Nope. Is it Brenda Cornwall?"

"Yep. It just came in from Frederick. He says it's current, taken just weeks ago."

Becky looked at the young girl with chestnut colored hair, azure-blue eyes, and a warm, friendly smile.

"Well, now we know what she looks like. At least we have something."

"We have more than the photo of Brenda."

"What else?"

Daniel sat up and reached into his blue jeans pocket. He pulled out a metal cylindrical tube with a push-button on one side and a slide lock latch.

"This belongs to my mother. I took it when you two were doing dishes." He handed it to her.

"What is it, some sort of flashlight?"

"No, I looked for one but couldn't find one. What you have in your hand is a defense weapon. It's pepper spray. My mother is licensed to have it. And with what we're facing, I know she wouldn't mind if I let you borrow it. Keep it on you tonight in case you need it."

"Licensed? You have to have a license for pepper spray?"

"Yeah. In the state of Massachusetts, you have to apply to get a pepper spray device. It's like a license to carry a gun. With my mom commuting to and from work in the city, I thought it best that she always have one in her handbag. And I'll put it back there tomorrow morning. Hopefully, it won't be needed."

An ice-cold shiver suddenly ran down Becky's spine while she anticipated what might be in store on this chilly, fall afternoon and evening.

"Did Frederick have anything else to say?"

"Not really, he's leaving New York shortly. He'll put the trash bag into the trunk of his black SUV and head for the Mass. Pike soon."

Just then Daniel's ring tone sounded. He began speaking. "Oh, yeah, hi, how are you doing? Oh really? Do you remember the time? Okay. Thanks for the heads up!"

Daniel hung up.

"Problems at work?" Becky asked.

"No, that was Gary Chan. He wanted to tell me he saw Marty Lane for the first time this morning. She was just leaving her apartment with a suitcase and her computer case in hand."

"Hmm. She's leaving for sure, and with no plans of returning."

"Gary told me she left her apartment about two hours ago. So, I bet she's already in Boston."

"Okay. Let's stop at some convenience store to pick up those cigarettes."

Later when they approached the North End and the Salem Street block, Daniel pulled his car over to park in an empty street curb space.

"The church is just a short walk from here, around the corner. Why don't we walk inside and make like we're touring with the rest of the visitors? If the guard isn't too watchful, you can try to get to that altar desk with the keys."

"Look, if you can distract him for a moment I can get near the altar, and I can get them, I think."

"I'll ask him to show me which way to get to the closest "T" station to get into Cambridge."

After the two stepped up the staircase, they showed the ticket-taker their student identification cards, entitling them to free admittance on Sundays.

They first mingled in the foyer reading some history material with other tourists. Then the two split off, heading toward the sanctuary and the altar of the Colonial church.

When Becky got within ten feet of the altar her eyes darted to the small, ornate desk. She then turned and gave Daniel a silent nod that she was ready to make her move.

Daniel reacted, stepping over toward the church guide. He turned so the older man's back was to the altar then politely asked the older man for directions. The man was cooperative but Daniel acted as if he didn't understand the instructions. This delay would give Becky more time. The guard politely led Daniel to the main doorway entrance. He pointed out how to walk to the nearest MBTA "T" station.

When Daniel returned inside, he saw Becky strolling along the side aisle windows, studying the architecture. He stepped through the pew boxes until he reached her.

She spoke in a whisper. "Good going keeping the guard's eye off of me. I did it! I got the key ring and already unlocked the side door!" she said when they met. "When the guard isn't looking again, we can scoot over to the stairway to the basement. Just follow me."

Daniel turned to face a discussion taking place at the back of the church.

"And that may happen soon! See that tour group from Ireland? They're approaching the church guard right now. I think they're asking him some questions."

"Okay, in one, two, three…let's go."

The two glided up to the altar and without stopping or looking back, opened the door leading down into the dark, creepy basement.

The damp, musty odor immediately hit them as they descended quietly. Becky still led the way as they stepped one step at a time down the antiquated stairs; careful not to make a sound. Only one light was lit, providing just a dim vision of the cellar.

As they carefully passed by the crypts filled with colonial skeletons, Daniel couldn't help but notice and read the text on the end of the burial boxes. Midway along the dirt floor, Becky stopped at a door, pointing to Daniel the thin slice of light coming from under the apartment door.

She tip-toed a short-distance past the apartment door. She spotted an old wooden door to her left. In the darkened area, she could barely make out the letters on the door. Using her bare hand, she wiped away the dust, revealing a white, handpainted message on the wooden boards.

No Admittance – Keep Out

Becky carefully tried the old iron door latch and nudged the door open. From the rusted hinges came a barely audible creaking sound. They both slipped behind the door not knowing what was in the room.

Inside there was no light. They could only feel each other's bodies for bearings in the small room.

"Wait! I have matches in my pocket," Daniel whispered. "I got them with the pack of cigarettes I bought."

He struck a match so they could look around. The tiny, flickering flame revealed that the room was lined with wooden shelves. Wooden crate boxes of varying sizes were set on them.

The first match died out before he struck a second one. Now they could both see that the boxes were filled with bones. Some were damaged bones of hands and feet, some of arms and legs. Stored higher up on the top shelf were the unmistakable human skulls of Colonist men, women, and children who had lived hundreds of years ago. An assortment of tools; hammers, saws, pliers, and other implements were scattered on the lowest shelf close to the ground floor.

Becky clung to Daniel. The two stayed frozen still, shocked at what they just discovered. There were skeleton parts surrounding them in the small, musty, old storage room.

After lighting the third match, Becky spotted a kerosene lantern. She grabbed it and opened the wick to be lit. After it flickered they could see more clearly the spiders crawling about, weaving their intricate webs.

Daniel took the old metal lantern from her, turning the wick down. He then set it on a shelf on the back wall of the room so the light couldn't be seen from the cellar hallway.

He then turned to Becky in a low whisper.

"Okay, now we have to see who the hell is inside of that apartment, Beck. I saw an overhead smoke alarm on one of the overhead floor joists. Let's take the cigarettes out of the package. But we have to keep one cigarette lit long enough for the alarm to go off."

"I've got an idea. What if we take the Parliament pack and pour a little kerosene on it from the lantern? Then we'll light just one cigarette near the filter and lay it on top of the pack. It should light and stay lit long enough for some smoke to set off the alarm."

"Okay. Are you ready for this?"

She took in a deep breath then exhaled. "I'm ready. Let's go!"

The two quietly left the storage room then tip-toed by the apartment door. There was a low volume radio music coming from inside. Adele's popular hit, "Set Fire to the Rain" was playing on the local Boston station. Daniel silently pointed upward to show Becky the smoke alarm with its tiny red, blinking light.

Just before setting the cigarette package on fire, Becky pointed to the naked light bulb hanging down.

"Daniel, loosen that bulb. I have an idea," she whispered.

He took a handkerchief from his rear pants pocket. He reached up and twisted the bulb until it went out.

After igniting the kerosene-soaked Parliament cigarette package and then the filtered butt, Daniel placed the two items on the dirt floor of the church basement. Set directly under the alarm, the smoke began to swirl and drift upward.

The two scampered back along the darkened hallway and slipped back into the storage room, carefully closing the door behind them.

They both exhaled and inhaled with tense breaths. They couldn't see very clearly but were alert for any sudden noises.

Within a minute, the smoke alarm blared out its loud, intermittent honking sound, doing its job to alert any occupants.

The next sound was that of the apartment door opening followed by Drew Lane's voice.

"What the hell's going on here? My God! It's the smoke alarm going off! What the hell caused that?"

"Something must be burning! I smell the smoke." The female voice belonged to Marty Lane.

Becky peeked outside of the storeroom. She couldn't see anything but smelled the acrid scent of smoke wafting around in the basement.

"Here, Drew, I have my lighter on me."

A cigarette lighter flickered next to the two Lanes' figures.

Becky could see the apartment door was left open with light coming from inside the secret residence.

"Oh, shit! Look, it's a lit butt, still burning on top of this empty cigarette package!" Drew said with an angry tone.

"Hey! What happened to the overhead light?" Marty asked.

"Damn it, Marty! You must have left this burning. How can you be so freakin' stupid? I told you never to smoke down here!"

"Hey! It wasn't me, I...."

"This pisses me off, Marty."

The next sound was a hand slapping the wall hard and echoing in the cellar hallway. The hard impact made the old wooden walls shake violently. With the dim lantern light, Becky saw the pine shelves shake. A human skull wobbled on the top shelf. It tipped from its resting place then fell down toward her head.

Daniel's quick reflexes reached up and caught the human skull just before it smashed down on top of her head.

With the skull firmly in his large hand, Daniel stared at it before replacing it on a lower shelf.

"For God's sake, Drew, you know me. I never smoke down here. I always go outside for a butt."

"Well, explain this empty package of Parliaments to me. You know I don't smoke. And, we're the only ones down here. I got it out now. Just wave your arms to stop the alarm noise. I'm gonna run upstairs to the supply closet and get a new light bulb. The church guard is long gone by now."

"Geez, don't get pissed at me! I don't know who left this butt burning. Maybe it was the guard from upstairs or one of the maintenance guys."

Becky heard Drew's footsteps climb up the wooden stairs. She turned to face Daniel then whispered.

"I'm gonna sneak into the apartment and hide. You get out of here, after they return back inside. I have a plan. I'll text you if Brenda is inside. If there's any trouble I'll let you know. If so, you can call the cops. At that point, it doesn't make any difference."

She barely discerned the worried expression on his face.

"Be careful. I'll leave after the two of them go back inside," Daniel whispered back.

Becky peeked around the corner and down the dark cellar hallway. She could only hear Marty's feet scuffling around on the dirt floor. Her waving arms worked; the obnoxious sound of the smoke alarm came to a stop.

Taking small steps, Becky moved quickly to the apartment doorway. With the door blocking Marty's view, she took a deep breath and slipped inside the hidden underground apartment.

CHAPTER TWENTY-SEVEN

After stepping over the entrance threshold and into the lighted kitchen, Becky reflected on Drew's tour.

That bastard was so proud when he showed off his underground apartment on the tour for us students. He gloated how he scored "free housing" as a college student.

The only addition to the kitchenette since the first visit was a black, vinyl trash barrel standing behind the door. The oversized barrel had a large pull handle at its rim and two large wheels at its base. Additionally, there were two neon-orange circle stickers affixed to its cover.

Hmm. It's just as Frederick told us. That's where the bag of five million is going to be dropped. And the orange stickers will make it stand out at nighttime so Frederick will notice it easily.

Without stopping, Becky glided directly into the small living room. She quickly peered around, looking for signs of life. She recalled the large, flat-screened TV. The sofa, now pulled out into a bed had a ball of disheveled bed sheets on top of it.

She tip-toed around the small room then peered into the bedroom but only found the bed covers were strewn about. Nobody was in there. There was no sign of Brenda or anyone else in the small basement residence.

Where the hell could she be? They must have her hidden inside here. I know I'm right.

Suddenly the sound of running water drew her eyes to the bathroom door. But the wooden door wasn't locked or closed tightly. When she looked down to the floor she saw the metal chain meandering along the carpet and leading into the bathroom. She couldn't wait any longer.

Her heart pounded. She stepped up to the door. But rather than knock, she grabbed the door handle and pulled it wide open.

Suddenly she was face to face with Brenda Cornwall.

For a silent moment the two girls simply stared at one another. But the girl standing in front of the bathroom sink was expressionless. There was no reaction in her eyes rimmed with deep circles of agony and despair. There was no life in those blue eyes, now bloodshot from calculated and administered narcotics.

It was apparent Brenda had just taken a shower with a large bath towel wrapped around her tiny body. Another smaller one was wrapped around her head to dry her hair.

Becky couldn't get her words out fast enough in a low whisper.

"Brenda. I'm gonna help you get out of here safely! But I have to hide before they come back. Where can I go?"

"Who are you?" the young girl asked, not particularly alarmed. Her monotone voice spoke of her listless energy, sapped from the drugs and incarceration forced upon her.

"Never mind that for now. Drew and Marty will be back in here soon!"

Brenda stepped out of the small bathroom. A heavy and thick metal cuff was locked on her left wrist.

With each step the shiny, metal chain attached to the cuff dragged behind her. She led Becky into the bedroom where the other end of the chain was fastened to a large eye-hook in the wall, tethering the hostage without any hope to escape.

The chain fit under the door. Brenda closed it behind her.

Brenda quickly sent a text to Daniel.

She's here. Get out of here when you can! Text later.

Becky's eyes panned around the spartan bedroom.

So they hid their kidnapped victim here in Drew's bedroom after leaving the hotel. And Drew must have been the one to sleep out on the living room sofa.

She stared intensely into the now frightened girl's bloodshot eyes and spoke to her in a low whisper.

"Brenda, my name is Becky Bing. I'm one of the scholarship students. I was supposed to be the girl to be kidnapped, before they nabbed you."

"Huh? What the hell does that mean?" Brenda asked in a dry, throaty whisper.

Before Becky could answer, the muffled sound of conversation could be heard. Drew and Marty had returned to the hidden underground apartment. The sounds of their footsteps stopped at the living room.

"Let me use the bathroom first, then I'll go in and check on her," Marty said.

Becky signaled for Brenda to lie down on the bed. The emotionally and physically drained victim followed the direction, pulling the sheets and bedcover up to her neck. She threw aside the towel wrap from her damp hair.

"Make like you're asleep!" Becky whispered.

Brenda closed her eyes while Becky slipped into the bedroom closet with bi-fold doors. She closed the door then pushed aside some hanging clothes to hide. She could still peer out through the narrow slotted door.

Within moments the sound of the bedroom door opening was followed by Marty's voice. Her low whisper was directed out toward Drew.

"Hey, she's out like a light. I'll come back in here later."

The door could be heard opening and closing once again.

"Okay. Let's go over the plans once again. We can't afford anything to go wrong."

Becky quietly slipped out of the closet.

Brenda's head popped up from the bed pillow. Becky signaled for her not to speak while she stepped to the bedroom door.

She leaned in with her ear close to the door to eavesdrop on the conversation taking place in the next room.

"Okay, Marty. As soon as it becomes darker outside, I'm going to wheel the trash barrel down the street. I told you where I'm leaving it on the opposite side from the church, and not too far from the Paul Revere statue. I'll set it so the orange stickers face the street, so they're visible. I'll hide in the souvenir store entranceway down the street. From there I'll call to let him know everything is ready. It'll be time to deliver the ransom money. From there, I can watch every step and the placing of the garbage bag into the trash barrel. And I can also watch him return to the base of the statue." Drew paused after his detailed plan.

"From there, you can make sure there are no cops snooping around, in case Cornwall contacted them," Marty added

"Yeah, but… I can only make sure he drops the trash bag inside. There could be anything inside that bag. After he goes to his place by the statue, as he was instructed, I'll go to the barrel and make sure it looks like five million bucks. But I sure as hell won't have time to count it."

"And while you're doing that, I'll be standing by the church entrance to wait before I come back here. My weapon is loaded and ready if needed."

"Good! Now, once it all looks good, I'll signal you with my flashlight. I'll flash it once—if it looks good. Then you come back here and get Brenda. But I'll flash it twice—if something looks wrong. And, if I send you two flashes, I want you to stay at the church entrance and wait."

Marty chuckled freely.

"It's just like you, my big brother, Professor Drew Lane, to add a twist of American History on a freakin' kidnap gig."

That little bit of information surprised Becky still with her ear pressed to the wall.

So the Lanes are brother and sister! And Drew is the older sibling.

"Now assuming the ransom money is all there, I'll give you the signal to go down, free up Brenda from the chain, and bring her outside."

"No sweat."

"While you're doing that, Marty, I'll wheel the trash barrel around the corner onto Hull Street where my Jeep is parked and waiting. I took the roof off. So, it's open. All we have to do is…jump in and get the hell away from here and drive to the Boss's house. The Boss won't be there as we know."

Becky was taking in the whole plan as she pressed her head closely against the thin wall separating the bedroom from living room.

My God! There are three of them! They have an accomplice driving the getaway car. I wonder who the hell this boss is. And I wonder where the boss is tonight? I hadn't planned on this.

She pulled out her cell and texted Daniel, while Brenda stood up from the bed.

There was a silent pause.

"Hey, what are you so worried about, bro'? It's all been planned out. We haven't made a mistake yet."

"I'm just nervous that the Cornwall parents may have made a bad decision and sent someone with him, or perhaps someone is following him. Or worse, maybe the FBI has been contacted. I want to be sure it looks all clear before you bring her up. I really don't want gunfire and a bloody turn to this."

"Don't worry. It'll just take me five minutes to come back down here, unlock her chain, and take her out of the church."

Inside the bedroom, Becky looked over at Brenda who was laying out a clean sweatshirt and jeans on top of the bed. She gave the drug-dazed girl the "shh" sign so she was careful not to make a noise. She resumed eavesdropping with her ear pressed to the door.

"Like I said," Drew continued. "I'll have the jeep running and we'll speed off to the boss's house. I'm just dropping off the money inside the front door. Fortunately, it's not far from there to Logan Airport."

"I won't go inside, Drew. You just drop the bag of money inside the house and we'll get the hell out of there. We can be inside the United Airlines terminal within twenty minutes."

"Yeah. The boss will handle the cash and wire some of it to the Bangkok National Bank. The account's already set up. We'll have access to it in two days."

"When do you think the boss will join us? We talked about maybe Thanksgiving."

"Perhaps. Hopefully it'll be sometime during the holidays or the new year. We want to make sure nothing becomes suspicious around here before the three of us are together once again."

Becky turned to look over once again at Brenda who had dropped her towels and was wearing only panties.

The topless and subdued teenager sat on the edge of the bed. With her back toward Becky, the hostage wiggled into a pair of blue jeans. She then picked up the oversized towel and draped it over her shoulders to modestly cover her breasts.

Becky realized it was impossible for Brenda to put on her bra or any top because of the lengthy chain locked at her wrist bracelet and tethered to the bedroom wall.

Becky pulled out her cell and texted Daniel.

There are three of them. Marty, Drew, and someone they call "the boss." I'll text again later.

"You know this was such a great plan, Drew! Nobody would ever expect our package, Brenda, would be hidden in the cellar of the Old North Church."

"Hey, it's a team effort. It took your cool acting performance, me with access to this apartment, and the boss with the detailed plans."

"Hey, we got some time to kill. I'm going out for some sandwiches. I'll go in and ask Brenda what she wants. You want your usual?"

"Why don't you get changed into your black duds before you go out? And I put the black stocking caps on the kitchen counter for later tonight."

"Okay. Let me check on our girl first."

Becky gave Brenda the "shh" signal once again as she quickly did an about face and scooted into the bedroom closet. She continued to listen as the bedroom door opened.

Marty entered the room and saw Brenda with only her blue jeans on, still clutching a bath towel.

"Okay, Brenda, let me free you up, so you can put on your bra and that sweatshirt of yours."

Marty plucked a key from her beige cargo pants and unlocked the metal cuff circling Brenda's wrist.

Brenda quickly put on her bra then slipped a sweatshirt over her head.

"Okay, back in your shackles, my friend," Marty said. "This is the last time. Next time I unlock you, it will be to let you go home."

"It can't come too quick to get away from you two assholes!"

Marty gave the victim a condescending look.

"So, what kind of sandwich do you want on your last night with us? I promise I won't be adding any drugs this time. It's your last few hours with us. Besides, nobody could hear you down here if you did yell out."

Becky peered through the louver-door slots. She could see the interaction but her view was limited.

"Just don't think you're getting away with this! My father will have the FBI on your asses before you know it," Brenda told her with forced strength in her voice.

"Ha! They'll never find us, and besides I'm sure your Pop doesn't want any more trouble." She headed for the door. "And I'll take that as a request for a chicken salad."

CHAPTER TWENTY-EIGHT

Becky once again quietly stepped out of the messy clothes closet. Socks and jerseys were strewn on the closet floor. She glanced over at Brenda who now had tears in her eyes.

"It's going to be all right," she whispered, draping an arm over the kidnapped girl. "We'll get you safely home one way or another."

"What are we going to do? You can't call the police, or they'll kill me. She has a gun you know," Brenda whispered back. "I've seen it many times."

"Listen, I have a friend, Daniel, who is working with me on this. Frederick knows about both of us. Right now I have to text Daniel."

Her fingers quickly tapped a message to start a texting conversation with her new boyfriend.

Where are you?

I'm outside now. Hidden across the street in an alley. R U all right?

I'm OK. Hiding in the BR with Brenda. Marty will be coming out soon to make a sandwich run.

I'll keep an eye out for her.

The getaway car is on corner of Hull St. It's an open Jeep.

I'll check it out! Hey, just saw Marty or someone come out the front door. Can't tell for sure. All dressed in black!

B careful! Still don't know who or where the 3rd person, the so-called BOSS, is tonight.

Text later.

Becky joined Brenda sitting on the edge of the bed.

"Becky, what did you mean when you told me that you were supposed to be the kidnap victim?"

The two spoke in a low whisper so that Drew couldn't hear them from the living room. Becky explained what had happened in New Haven and at the scholar's conference that Brenda never attended.

Then it was Brenda's turn to tell her story.

"Marty met me at the Hotel parking garage. She told me she was Samantha Rawlings from Indiana. I was pulling my suitcase behind me and the next thing I knew, a man's voice called out my name. Then someone, I think Marty, put a handkerchief over my face that was doused with something medicinal. I went out like a light."

"Did you see who the man was?"

"Not then, but when I woke up in Marty's hotel room, I saw that he had the adjacent room. I still didn't know what had happened. They chained me to the hotel furniture and taped my mouth shut. Sometimes Marty left me alone, as she dressed up like a blonde woman in business clothes. But most times she stayed in the room with me. We had two double beds in the room."

"Brenda, we heard Marty refer to a third person, 'the Boss'. Do you have any idea who the Boss is?"

"Hell, no! The few times I was lucid, I only saw Drew and Marty. They're brother and sister you know."

Becky nodded. "Look, I could call the cops right now. But it would blow the whole thing. Who knows what they would do to you if it went bad? But as soon as I can get you out of here, I'm making the call. You don't think Frederick would do anything crazy, do you?"

Brenda paused before answering.

"I…I don't think so. He's been with the family for over twenty years and very loyal. But at the same time, he's extremely secretive. I don't know that much about him personally. I think if my folks told him to hand over the ransom money, get me, and take me home, that's what he will do."

Becky paused, staring into the weakened teen's eyes.

"So you're telling me we can trust him."

"Huh! Ah…sure, we can trust Frederick. I mean, I don't think there's any reason not to trust him. Besides, what other option do we have?"

Brenda watched as Becky's face contorted into a frown.

"What's the problem, Becky?"

"It's just that I still haven't figured out who the third person might be in this kidnapping case. We know how Drew and Marty are connected but I can't imagine someone else involved."

"Yeah, me too! Are you thinking that Frederick might be involved?"

Becky got up from the bed and paced around the bedroom.

"It's just that Frederick called me…or my friend, to tell us about the kidnapping. He told us how your father and mother were working on it to get the cash right away. Then Frederick calls telling us your father took ill with heart problems and that he would be handling the transfer of money. It just seems so convenient that…"

The sudden sound of Marty's voice echoing in the next room could be heard.

"Okay, bro'. I got you the best meatball 'spucky' in the Italian North End with your favorite drink, a coffee frappe. Now, let me go in and give our 'golden goose' her sandwich. By the way, she's getting a little bitchy now. I liked her better when we had her stoned. Be right back!"

Becky retreated quickly back into the clothes closet. But when she tried to close the bi-fold door, it became stuck half way on something on the floor. She slid to the side of the closet, hiding behind Drew's clothes hanging from the closet rod.

Marty breezed into the bedroom.

"Here, Brenda. I got you a chicken salad on a roll and a pink lemonade. It'll give you energy for your long night ahead. You know how long the ride back to Westchester is going to be!"

Brenda ignored the wrapped sandwich set on top of the bed cover.

"Hey, what the hell happened to my own car? Is it still in the hotel parking garage?"

"Huh? Oh, no, girl! Since we had your car keys, we took it for a very long ride. Nice wheels though. I had never driven a hot, BMW Z4 before. I had fun with it until I had to get someone to take care of it. It's probably been sold three times by now. And God only knows where it is today."

Marty turned to leave and noticed the closet door partially opened. She slowly stepped over to it, her eyes riveted on the clothes on the hangers. Just inches from the closet, Marty quickly dropped down, bending her knees.

Becky's heart pounded in her chest, anticipating Marty seeing her jeans and athletic shoes while she stooped at the low level. With nervous perspiration beading quickly on her forehead, she stared down at the kneeling Marty. The thin, white surgical scar on the back of her pale white neck was, once again, clearly visible.

All of a sudden, there was a forceful yanking at the bottom of the closet door. Then the bi-fold doors slammed shut.

"There I got it! Hey, Brenda, we'll have to tell Drew to become more 'ship-shape'. One of his socks on the closet floor jammed the door open!"

"It's not my job, bitch!"

"Okay, see ya!"

The bedroom door slammed. Becky stood frozen in the closet, catching her breath.

"Becky, are you all right?" Brenda whispered, opening the bi-fold door.

She stepped out from behind the clothes.

"Man, that was close!" Becky answered in a low voice.

Becky's cell vibrated. Daniel was texting.

Frederick called. He's not far from the North End. He'll pull up on Salem Street at eleven. Then dump the bag of money. Told me he's wearing all black even a black stocking cap as instructed by the caller.

Becky replied with a text message.

Did you find the Jeep parked on Hull Street?

Daniel replied quickly.

Yes. But it won't be going far with four flat tires. My Swiss Army knife came in handy.

Becky smiled at what Daniel had done. Deflating tires was a smart thing. *Of course, as soon as Drew sees the flat tires, he'll know something is wrong. But if my guess is right, it'll be too late.*

Becky sat on the bed next to Brenda. She couldn't hide her anxiety and troubled expression.

"What's wrong, Becky," she whispered.

"Frederick is wearing the same outfit as Drew and Marty. All three are in black sweatshirts, black pants, and a black wool stocking cap."

Brenda immediately became quiet.

CHAPTER THIRTY

The quiet of the night grew heavy inside the underground apartment.

Brenda paced back and forth inside the bedroom carrying her shiny chain.

Becky sat near the closet door, in case someone should suddenly come in. Each watched the alarm clock on the nightstand change its neon digits until it finally became eleven o'clock.

The stillness was finally broken with Marty's voice shouting out from the living room.

"Hey, Brenda, make sure you're ready in ten minutes! Drew's already into his position about now, and I'll be back down shortly. We'll have to move fast right after I unhook you."

Becky texted Daniel.

It's beginning now.

He replied instantly.

I know. I saw Drew come out. Frederick's opening the back of his SUV. I can't see it, but I hear him pulling on the plastic garbage bag.

Becky tapped quickly.

Daniel—watch out for him!

Brenda looked at Becky nervously. She spoke again in a whisper.

"I just hope nobody gets hurt. I mean, like you and Daniel. You know, the ransom money doesn't mean that much to my family. They could have asked for much more, but it would take a lot more garbage bags."

"Don't worry, Brenda. We'll get everyone out of this safely except for those who'll get a long jail sentence; the Lane brother and sister!"

Brenda stared at Becky before responding.

"And the boss. Let's not forget…the boss."

A text came in again from Daniel. Becky tilted her cell phone so Brenda could read the message.

Bag of money was dropped. Drew now checking it out. Frederick stands at the statue. A light from flashlight went off on and off.

Becky quickly texted back.

One flash or two?

Just one.

Brenda looked over at Becky as she slipped the cell back into her front jeans pocket.

"She's coming for me. You better hide."

Becky looked at the girl beside her. She leaned in and gave her a quick bear hug.

"Good luck, Brenda."

"Thanks, and ah, same to you, Becky!"

Becky stepped into the closet, closing the bi-fold door.

The noise of footsteps moving quickly down the steps echoed through the rooms.

Moments later, the bedroom door swung open.

"Okay, Brenda, here we go. It's game time!"

Becky could see Marty quickly unlock the chained wrist bracelet, grab Brenda by the arm, and forcibly escort her out of the room.

She texted to Daniel with her update. There was no reply.

She texted him again but there was still no response.

I have to kill some time here. I can't go up until it's safe. C'mon Daniel, let me know what the hell's going on!

She sat on the bed visualizing what might be going on outside of the legendary church.

Drew must be wheeling the barrel of money to the car parked on Hull Street. He might even be there now, pissed at the four flat tires. Marty must have turned Brenda over at the base of the statue.

Suddenly her cell vibrated with a text from Daniel. She pulled the device from her jeans pocket.

Brenda has been released to Frederick. They are already driving away. Money bag's now in back of Jeep. Drew just found out he has flat tires. Here comes someone dressed in black stocking cap. I don't think it's Marty. Subject came from a different direction than from the Old North Church.

Becky texted back to him.

Call police 911 NOW!

There was no reply.

Becky looked at her watch. It was almost midnight. Her mind raced, trying to think what she could do without creating a scene and interfering with Daniel getting help to come to the historic Boston street.

I'd better get the hell out of here now. I can go upstairs to the main church and maybe peek outside to see what's going on. When I know the cops are on scene, I can run out of here.

She ran up the dark set of stairs. Within minutes, she was up at the church altar tip-toeing around. She used her iPhone flashlight to navigate down the darkened church aisle. When she reached the main entranceway doors, she stepped to one side, finding a small window through which she could peek out.

But there were no sirens or police cruiser strobe lights. It was just pitch black in a dark corner of the quiet colonial city at midnight on a Sunday night.

Then something unexpected happened. Something suddenly appeared. But it wasn't any bright blinking lights. And it wasn't the loud sound of a police cruiser's siren that Becky sensed wafting in from behind.

It was an aromatic scent. Becky smelled something now that hadn't been inside the church before. It was a scent she had never smelled before, until…she had come to the Boston conference. She remembered it was a unique fragrance, made locally. The scent had a name, "Nantucket Breeze."

Becky turned to face a figure dressed in black pants, black sweatshirt, and a black stocking cap. The face could barely be made out with the dim emergency lights inside the church hallways. But the intruder carried more than a refreshing, salty, beach scent. Gripped in an outstretched hand with barrel pointing at Becky's face was a nine-millimeter gun.

"So we meet again, Miss Becky Bing."

Becky gulped, looking straight into the barrel of the handgun.

"And you. You're the one they call the boss," she managed to get out.

"I am the boss. I'm always the boss."

Brooke Gleason flashed a quick but confident smile as she stood only two feet away from Becky.

"You won't get away with this, Brooke!"

"Why not? Nobody knows what's going on here yet. Frederick will speed away to Westchester to get Brenda back home. He's too afraid to call the cops. See, Becky, you should have read my little note I snuck into your hotel room. I wanted you to return to Connecticut before all this happened. You know, you could have avoided all this if you had left town when you were supposed to return home."

"If you haven't guessed by now, I don't take hints very well. And I do my own thing—always by myself."

"I figured as much when I saw the flat tires on Drew's Jeep. I thought it might be you who was involved. And I figured you came up here to hide after killing the tires. You chose to stay behind for the weekend and I figured you must have sensed something was going on with Marty acting as Brenda. And, you were on Drew's tour when he showed you kids his little apartment downstairs. You put the pieces of the puzzle together."

"So I was always on your radar screen, eh?"

"I never was keen on you, Becky. You were our first target, but caused us all problems from the beginning. After Marty saw that you were Chinese-American, it became too risky to impersonate you. Someone could have known or found out that you were Asian before the scholar's conference began. So we abandoned Plan A and went to plan B. Brenda was risky too, because of Mr. Cornwall's influence, but we scared the bejesus out of him, telling him his daughter would have a painful death up here in Boston if he didn't cooperate."

"So, now what?"

"It's very simple. You thought you could pull this off by yourself, Becky, but apparently no cops are coming, so we just go back to Plan A," Brooke replied.

"Back to Plan A?"

"Yeah. I'm taking you with me. We'll slip out the side door to my car a few blocks from here. Then we pick up Drew and Marty. After they take the early morning flight out of the country, I'll begin my own negotiations with your parents back in Connecticut. It will be a simple deal—you return home alive for five million bucks or you return dead. Pretty simple, eh?"

Becky paused as anticipation hung in the stale air of the old church.

Just then, the buzzing sound of Becky's cell broke the silence. Becky knew it was Daniel's text coming in.

"Oh, Becky. You won't need to take that cell phone. Hand it over to me. I'll answer it!

Shit, Brooke could respond to Daniel telling him anything, just like they did with Brenda's cell. They texted to the Cornwall parents making like the messages were sent from their daughter. God! I gotta do something...quick!

Becky gripped her cell phone then reached out to hand it off to Brooke Gleason. But instead of putting it in her palm, she intentionally dropped it on the church floor.

"Goddamnit! Pick it up, Becky!"

Becky slowly bent her knees, lowering down toward the floor where it was much darker. While she picked up the phone with her left hand, her right hand reached into her jeans pocket and felt the narrow canister of pepper spray.

As she slowly stood up, she fingered the safety latch to open on the cylindrical weapon.

She handed the cell to Brooke's opened empty hand, the other still holding the gun aimed at her.

With one swift motion she lifted up the tube and sprayed Brooke several times directly into her eyes. At the same time she crouched down and bolted down the church hallway.

The shots of pepper spray surprised and stunned Brooke with intense pain.

"Oh you little freakin' bitch! Ugh! I can't see, I can't see!"

The next sound was more comforting for Becky. It came from the police cruisers' blaring sirens now filling Salem Street. Her body pushed the crash bar on the door. She was soon standing outside on the staircase of the Old North Church. Her own eyes smarted from the intensity of the pepper spray. Tears flowed from her eyelids.

"Are you all right, Miss?" yelled a uniformed BPD sergeant coming up the granite stairs.

"Yeah, but go inside and get Brooke Gleason. She's got a gun on her and is escaping. Watch the side door!"

Other cops ran into the church, while others ran to the side door.

The cop carefully escorted Becky down to his cruiser and helped her get into the back seat. When she finally opened her blurry and burning eyes wide, she noticed someone already sitting beside her. It was her new best friend, Daniel Yang.

Becky collapsed into his opened arms and snuggled tightly into his hard body. Daniel produced a handful of tissues and began wiping away her burning tears. By the time they got to the Boston Police station her pain had subsided and her eyesight was almost back to normal.

* * *

They waited inside the Boston Police Department interview room for nearly twenty minutes before two detectives, one male and one female, came inside to speak to them.

Before they started, the uniformed sergeant at the church stepped in and brought them up to date.

"Just to let you know, we already have the Lane brother and sister in custody. We found them hiding on Hull Street, near the plastic trash bag filled with the ransom money. Daniel had tipped us off at your direction, Becky, and we responded quickly and quietly.

"He then directed us into the church. After you told us about Gleason, we caught her trying to escape through the side door. She was in bad shape from your pepper spray. We confiscated her handgun and cuffed her. They're all under arrest and the FBI is now joining the investigation interview."

"Brooke Gleason was the missing piece I never knew about," Becky commented.

The sergeant closed the door and paced down a corridor. The female detective brought them back into their objective.

"Okay, we all might as well get comfortable and get to your statement, Becky. And Daniel, you can chime in with anything you want as her story unfolds. We will tape record the session.

"So first of all, where did this kidnap case begin?"

Becky took a long swig from her bottle of iced tea.

"Well, Detective, it really began back in my hometown in Connecticut, just outside of New Haven. I got a surprise call from a student scholar who had green hair, and…."

28295317R00131

Made in the USA
Lexington, KY
13 December 2013